HOUSE OF JUDGES

USA TODAY BESTSELLING AUTHOR

KEARY TAYLOR

HOUSE OF JUDGES

THE HOUSE OF ROYALS SAGA
BOOK FOUR

KEARY TAYLOR

First Edition: June 2016

Taylor, Keary, 1987-

House of Judges (House of Royals) :

a novel / by Keary Taylor. – 1st ed.

ALSO BY KEARY TAYLOR

THE BLOOD DESCENDANTS UNIVERSE

House of Royals Saga

House of Royals

House of Pawns

House of Kings

House of Judges

House of Ravens

Garden of Thorns Trilogy

Garden of Thorns

Garden of Snakes

Garden of Graves

Crown of Death Saga

Crown of Death

Crown of Blood

Crown of Ruin

Crown of Bones

Blood Rose Nights

Born Reckless

Born Savage

Born Chaos

Born Wicked

PARALLEL VERSE GUARDIANS

A Shadow in the Light

A Glimmer in the Night

A Spark in the Ash

RESURRECTING MAGIC SERIES

Rise of the Mage

Keeper of the Lost

Shadow of the Locked

Academy of the Found

THE FALL OF ANGELS TRILOGY

Branded

Forsaken

Vindicated

Afterlife (the novelette companion to Vindicated)

Returned (ten year anniversary follow up)

THE EDEN TRILOGY

The Raid (An Eden Short Story)

The Bane

The Human

The Ashes (an Eden Short Story)

The Eve

THE NERON RISING SAGA

Neron Rising

Neron Skies

Nero Awakening

Nero Blood

Nero Nights

Neron Wars

Nero Kingdom

THREE HEART ECHO

TO LOVE A McCAIN

Ever After Drake

Moments of Julian

Depths of Lake

Playing it Kale

WHAT I DIDN'T SAY

Also by T.L. Keary (thriller/suspense pen name)

OUR LAST CONFESSION

SKIN AND BONE

CHAPTER ONE

JUST A FEW DAYS AGO, I was a queen.

Just days ago, I had two mansions full of immortal Born vampires ready to follow me to the ends of the earth.

Days ago, I killed a poor girl whose only crime was being in the wrong place at the wrong time.

Days ago, the one man I thought would be loyal to me until the end of my days left me.

Just days ago, I was framed.

Just a few days ago, I thought I was going to die.

Just a few days ago, everything fell apart.

And now, I burn.

THE SUN BLAZED THROUGH THE spring air, shining over a beautiful little town tucked away in a valley in the mountains of Austria. It warmed the dew that had collected overnight. It coaxed spring flowers up toward the light. It grew the spring crops that would feed the residents.

It then finds its way into a small hole in the ceiling above me. It reflects and intensifies, zigzagging downward through the mirrored tube leading into a stone and steel prison. Before it reaches me.

I cower in a corner, my body curled into a small ball, my knees pressed against two of the steel walls. My elbows rest on my thighs, my hands pressed hard into my eye sockets. My entire body quakes, aware of the blinding light at my back. Pain laces into every muscle of my body. Fiery sparks shoot through my eyes, despite their covering, exploding into my brain, tearing down the back of my neck, sending the alert to the rest of my changed, immortal body.

A choked off sob escapes my throat.

Just a few days ago, I was a queen.

"It will be dark soon," a voice calls from the next cell. "Deep breaths. Try not to move." He takes a sharp, hissing, deep breath. His own agony is so apparent. "It will be dark soon."

This is a prison, and its inmates are all vampires.

I want to respond. To agree—that it will be dark soon. To acknowledge the encouraging words he's been offering all day. But I can't move. I can't breathe. If I do, my entire body will alight into flames and I will be nothing but a pile of ash on the stone floor.

I reside in a prison, and the sun is my tormentor.

"Two cups of warm water," I breathe out through the pain. "Yeast. A teaspoon of sugar. Salt. Honey. Five cups of flour." I start rattling off the ingredients to the first recipe that comes to mind—my mother's homemade pizza crust dough. "Water. Yeast. Sugar, salt, honey. Flour."

In my mind, I'm kneading the dough. I'm flattening it into shape. I'm watching my mother's hands as a seven-year-old. There's flour all over the floor, a smear of it on Mom's cheek. And smiles on both of our faces.

I'm back in the old bakery, it's five in the morning and I'm just finishing the blueberry scones. Mrs. Kachinski is standing outside the doors, waiting for us to open so she can get her morning coffee and muffins. The snow is softly falling outside, and the mountains of Colorado are barely visible through the dark.

But I'm *not* there. I'm cowering on the floor. I'm quaking in pain and fear.

"It'll be dark soon," I breathe to myself.

I FEEL THE SUN RECEDE, one ray at a time. It drops behind the horizon, the darkness creeping in one tiny inch at a time. Marginally, my cell grows from one shade of gray to the next. And finally, I feel the dark take over with a loving, comforting embrace.

And I collapse onto the floor.

A collective sigh rushes from several of the other prisoners. Followed by loud cursing from the German speaker.

For the first time in twelve hours, I open my eyes. Everything is a grayish yellow haze with a halo of light clouding my vision. I blink several times, attempting to clear it, but it doesn't go away.

"You'll be able to see again in about ten minutes," he says from the next cell.

His voice causes a catch to snag in my chest. I bite my lower lip, attempting to gain control of something fast and fierce beneath my skin.

He takes a deep breath. "You okay?"

His voice is the bandage ripped off. The heat applied too quickly to the glass. My tipping point.

The breath rips in and out of my chest, at first in a hiccup. And then faster and faster, until it develops into a sob.

"I'm so sorry, Ian," I cry as I lie on my back, on the hard, stone floor. "I'm so sorry."

"Hey," I hear him say; his voice sounds uncomfortable. "Don't... Don't say that. You didn't..."

But he can't finish his sentence, because there's so much that I *did*. That he did. That we never were together.

I curl into a ball once again and roll onto my side as I let the tears silently consume me.

• • •

HE DOESN'T TRY TO TALK to me, and for that, I am grateful. But I can tell, I just can, that he's every bit aware of me as I am of him. Of every breath. Of every step taken across the tiny space. Of every blink.

But we don't say a word.

What would I say? Where would I even start?

Footsteps demand my attention as they come down the narrow passageway that drops down into the prison. Two of them. Down the aisle.

I scramble to my feet, righting my clothes, wiping my face clear of the tears and dirt and humiliation. I hold my chin high as metal screeches against metal and the door slides open just a bit.

Trinity stands there, a guard just behind her. For a second, I debate if I can overtake him, make a break for it. But there's not a chance. I couldn't even find my way out of the castle.

"Hey," Trinity offers. She takes a step forward, into the cell, and the guard slides the door closed. He locks us in.

"Are you okay?" I ask, searching her over for signs of damage. Her hair is still as unwashed as ever, her nose ring gleaming in the dark. Her black clothes are unrumpled.

"I'm fine," she says, and the words come out rather grudgingly. She doesn't want me to care about her, but for some reason, I do. She even gives me a little glare. "They put me up in a room. Sent me a feeder. I'm fine."

I nod, still looking her over for signs of distress. The

only ones there are seem to be directed at me. "You're sure?" I ask in relief.

She's having a hard time looking me in the eye, but she does meet my gaze for just a moment, nodding, before her eyes dart away. "You don't look so good."

My first instinct is to tell her what she can go do to herself, but then I remember that I am a prisoner here, and she volunteered to be my escort. "Been a while since I've seen the sun. Our reunion was a complicated one."

Trinity swears under her breath, and her eyes instantly find the light tube. "Some prison," she says.

"Is there any word on my trial?" I ask. "What are they planning to do with me?"

She doesn't look back at me with my question, but continues to stare at the tube that leads out into the dark night. "I haven't heard anything yet. The way they were talking last night after they dragged you off, I don't think they're in a hurry to deal with you. You could be here for a while."

My heart races faster with each word she offers. My memory goes back to last night, when I sat tied to a chair, eating at the dinner table as if I were a guest. Until someone grabbed me from behind and started dragging me off into the dark underbelly of the castle.

"What about..." My breath catches in my chest. And a sweat breaks out onto my palms. Because everyone can hear everything in this prison. Especially the man in the cell next to mine. But I have to know. "What about Raheem? Is he okay?"

Trinity gives me a funny look, not understanding the way I'm acting because of my question. "A couple of guards hauled him out of the dining hall pretty quick after they took you away. He was freaking out. Screaming in some language I didn't even recognize. One of the King's people jabbed something into his neck, though, and knocked him out."

Now, it's my turn to swear. I turn away from Trinity, my hands fisting in my hair. I squeeze my eyes closed and try to calm down the angry tiger rearing its head inside of me.

"He's too valuable to the King," I say, mostly to myself. "He won't kill Raheem. He can't."

"I don't know," Trinity says. "He didn't seem too pleased to find out his favorite spy was sneaking around behind his back with his favorite maybe-resurrected queen."

And all the blood in my resurrected body drops into my feet before disappearing all together.

There. She's put it out there, for anyone in this prison to hear.

I swallow hard.

"Thank you, Trinity," I say through gritted teeth. "I do hope you'll come back with more updates later."

She gives me a look, but she's met with my own deathly one. Recognizing the command to leave, she knocks on the steel door twice. The guard opens it, and with one last look over her shoulder, she walks out.

I beg for their footsteps to retreat more slowly. I don't want to look Trinity in the eye any more, but I pray for them not to leave me alone with the giant elephant in the prison. But in just a few seconds, the sounds of their shoes on the stones are gone, and all is quiet again.

One silent beat. Two.

A full silent minute that feels like a vampire eternity.

"Don't you have anything to say?" I finally breathe.

Ian lets out a sigh. I hear him shift, sitting on the stone floor and rests his head against the steel wall. "Nope, not really."

"Really?" I challenge him. I sink to the floor, resting myself against the very same wall Ian sits against.

"Really," he says. Tight. Sharp.

"You're so full of shit sometimes, Ian," I say, letting out a slow breath.

"Yeah, well, you wrote the book on how to stuff the turkey," he shoots back.

"You know, you keep acting like all of this is my fault," I bite. "That I brought this on the both of us. But you seem to keep forgetting that we were both *born* this way."

Ian lets out a disgusted sigh, and I hear him climb to his feet. "You should really just go the hell back to Silent Bend. Things have been a lot less dramatic around here in the last month without you around."

"You're calling me a drama queen?" I screech back. I climb to my feet as well, facing the wall, yelling at it. "Look at you, acting all typical Ian Ward—in denial of reality!" I throw my arms up in the air, behind me, and take a bow to the wall.

Someone yells at us in German and the Spanish speaker lets out a string of curse words at us.

"Stay the hell out of this!" Ian and I both somehow shout at the same time.

"You're freaking unbelievable," I mutter under my breath. My heart cracks a little further, and I hate myself for that.

"Me?" he hisses. "What about you, Alivia? We were... We had... And now, I hear you've already moved on, well and good, sleeping around with someone when the King might have killed you for it."

"At least Raheem doesn't *hate* me for something I couldn't do anything about!" I scream. I rush that wall and smack both my palms against it, sending a bolt of pain racing through my hands.

"I never hated you!" he spits. "I hate this freaking system, this bloody race. And you just ran towards it, blindly, with open arms!"

My mouth drops open in disbelief. "You are an ignorant idiot, Ian Ward! You talk about bravery and making your own fate, but you turn a blind eye to anything different than *your* black and white version of right and wrong."

"Apparently, you don't know the difference yourself," he seethes. "You're here in prison!"

"I could have left," I say through clenched teeth. "I was going to escape. But Elle asked me where you were, and I couldn't walk away from her. I let them take me for her. For you."

And that finally turns him silent. Ian would do anything for his sister. She was the last person he expected to come up in this conversation.

"So yeah, Ian," I say, kicking him while he's down for a beat. "I went into Raheem's arms willingly. I went to someone who embraced everything I was, all the good I was trying to do, despite my circumstances. Because you turned your back on me. Time and time again. I'm a Royal, Ian. I have to act like one. I'm not the moldable, lost little child you keep treating me as."

And maybe I've hit the right nerve, because finally, for the first time in maybe ever, Ian doesn't have anything to say in response.

CHAPTER TWO

ONE DAY OF BURNING. ONE night of utter silence. Five screaming prisoners.

The sun rises and sets four times. Five. Six. And Ian and I do not say another word.

The air grows thicker and thicker by the minute, just a little more pressure. Just a little more pain added to the mix. But all the more pride set upon our chests, making it harder to breathe and harder to offer the first word.

But I refuse to back down. Ian needs to recognize he's being far too self-righteous. That this life of ours has never been black and white. He needs to accept reality.

Ian's silence tells me he's not forgiving anything, either.

So we go another one—two days in utter silence. Except for the screams of pain during the day.

And with each passing day, I fear I'm losing another

piece of my mind. All I can think about is the burn in the back of my throat. The dehydration taking over my body. The growl in my belly, begging for food. I haven't been offered an ounce since stepping foot in the prison.

I'm slowly starving. Dehydrating. I'm not sure if it's a blessing or a curse, though, that it won't kill me.

On the ninth day of imprisonment, I hear footsteps coming down the stairs. Heavy boots, worn by a heavy body. The sound of chains rattle through the air. Past the first cell. Past the next. Down the aisle before they stop at my own cell.

The sound of a key grates against steel and the lock pops open at the same time my heart leaps into my throat. The door slides open and I'm greeted by a hard-faced man with a beard that touches his chest. A thick scar runs down one side of his face. And there's a smear of blood on his lower lip.

"Hands," he says in a thick German accent. He holds up a set of handcuffs with a link of chain between them.

I swallow once before holding my hands up, bringing my wrists together. The guard secures the inch-thick bands around my wrists before snapping a similar pair around my ankles.

"Liv?" Ian suddenly calls out, a hint of worry showing in his voice.

"It's okay," I assure him, my heart suddenly racing. "It'll be okay."

The guard yanks on one end of the chain, dragging me

forward. My weakened body isn't prepared for the force of it. A little yelp instinctually leaps from my throat as I stumble forward.

"Liv!" Ian yells again. I hear his hands smack against the steel door as we walk past it.

"I'm okay!" I yell to him. "I—"

But I'm cut off when we reach the stairs and I'm being dragged up them.

"Try anything funny and you'll regret it," the guard says. I look to the side, where he stands, and see he holds a stake securely in one hand.

"Nothing funny," I promise him. I study the huge arm muscles. The thick ropes of strength that wrap around his chest, even climb up his neck. This man could crush me with one hand. He could drive that stake clean through my chest and pop it out the other side.

My body has physically weakened in the time I've been here. I couldn't fight him, and I'm sure that was designed on purpose.

I have little doubt that he has been given orders to kill me if necessary. Since Cyrus has confirmed I am not the queen, he has no need to keep me around.

I wonder briefly what will happen to my House should I die here in *Roter Himmel*. Silent Bend will once again be without a Royal leader. It will once again fall into poverty and discord.

No, I tell myself. That won't happen. I will get out of

this framed mess. I will return to the people who need me.

Up and up a thousand stairs. Down hallways. Down another set of stairs. Across a huge ballroom. Winding up a spire. It feels as if we've been walking for an hour. When, finally, we stop at a massive, ancient wooden door.

The guard knocks on the door five times, one long and four quick raps on the wood. "You don't have long; use the time wisely."

I'm about to ask him what he means, but the door suddenly opens, and my eyes meet Raheem's beautiful ones.

"Thank you, Mads," Raheem says as he takes the chains from the guard, who also offers a key. "We'll be quick."

My mouth hangs open, speechless as I shuffle inside. Raheem closes the door behind us and makes quick work of removing my chains.

"I am sorry for these," he says as the shackles on my wrists fall to the floor and he sets to work removing the ones on my ankles. "We had to be careful in case you were seen. You are a prisoner, and I didn't want this looking suspicious."

The bands fall from my ankles, and Raheem rises to his full height, his dark eyes studying me.

And the openness there, the worry and the underlying anger, they cause the very fragile wall I've built around myself in protection to crumble and fall.

My arms fly to Raheem's neck, wrapping myself against him. My body molds to his as his arms come around me, clinging hard and tight.

"I'm here, my *nofret*," he breathes into my neck.

"What happened?" I ask as tears pool in my eyes. "After they took me away. Did they hurt you?"

I back away just slightly so I can study him. He seems to be in one piece, no bruises, no missing limbs. He wears his usual tunic and matching pants, a black keffiyeh on his head.

"They didn't appreciate my final break of secrecy," he says as a smile cracks in one corner of his mouth. He brings his hands up to either side of my face, cradling me so gently. "I've been banned from the presence of the King until further notice, but no, they did not do anything to me."

A relieved sigh escapes me, and I collapse forward into his chest, my cheek resting against him as my arms wrap around him once more. "I've been so terrified."

"You needn't worry about me," he whispers into the top of my head, his lips brushing there. "Have they been treating you fairly?"

I shrug, shaking my head. "They're just leaving me down in the prison to rot," I mumble against the soft fabric of his shirt. "There's been no word. Nothing for over a week."

He lets out a noise of displeasure. "I'm afraid they will take their time," he says. "In the King's long lifeline, he's never in a hurry for anything, unless it is Sevan." He lets me go and crosses the room to the kitchen area. He opens a fridge and takes something out. "Here," he says, extending it toward me. "You need this."

The moment I realize it's a blood bag, I'm across the room in a single heartbeat, my fangs dripping. I tear into it, the cold liquid cascading down my parched throat. When I finish it in less than ten seconds, Raheem hands me another.

"It's one of their favorite tactics," he says as he hands me a third. "Dehydration. You get thirsty enough and you'll confess to anything for five drops of blood."

"So they will try to convict me, even if I am innocent?" I ask as I drag the back of my hand over my mouth, wiping away the remaining drops.

"You mustn't underestimate the King's brutality," Raheem says, his brows furrowing. "He's an addict. Even if it isn't logical, even if the truth is staring him in the face, if he needs a fix, he will get it."

The weight of that sends me back a step. My foot catches something, and I sink down into a chair. I know this. I've been witness to it. Antonia. Micah. Jasmine. Over a dozen Bitten.

I've toyed with the King. I made him believe I was his queen, finally returned to him after 271 years. His thirst for my blood will be strong.

"I'm not ready to die," I breathe to myself.

Raheem comes to crouch in front of me. He brings a

hand to my cheek, forcing me to look him in the eye. "You are innocent. Of this, I know. And of this, your House knows."

"No," I counter, shaking my head. "They don't. They think I did this."

"Not all of them," he says. "I've been in contact this entire time with Dr. Jarvis. They are working tirelessly to gather evidence in your favor."

My lower lip quivers as the tears that have been pooling in my eyes break free. "They are?"

He nods. "You haven't lost them all, Alivia."

I sniff, looking away from him as I wipe the tears from my face. I don't want to be this crying, terrified girl. But everything has been taken away. I am stripped to the bare bones. And I am left with very, very little.

"Why don't you go take a shower?" Raheem says as he stands. "Eat something. We don't have long before someone might come looking for you, but we do have a few minutes."

I nod, letting the numb fog take me over once again at the thought of returning to the prison. I climb to my feet and head for the door Raheem points to across the room. Behind it, I find a massive bathroom.

Black walls stretch high and grand. Two chandeliers hang from the ceiling. Red accents are splashed here and there, highlighted by gold. Absentmindedly, I peel my disgusting clothes off, taking in the grandness of it all.

Movement to my left catches my eye, and I turn to

find a mirror. Huge in size, floor to ceiling, rimmed in intricate gold patterns. But it's myself I can't look away from.

Already, my body looks thinner. My arms spindlier. The gap between my thighs growing wider. My cheekbones more prominent. The change would probably be unnoticeable to human eyes, but to my enhanced vampire ones, it's certainly there.

But it's the veins that draw my attention first. Black, inflamed veins spread around my eyes, tracing down my cheeks, stretching toward my neck. Before just a few minutes ago, it had been over a week since I'd last had blood. I'm still practically a newborn vampire. I have to feed. Or I begin to waste away.

As I study myself, though, I see the blackness begin to dissipate, easing back. My body has been fed, sated for the moment.

I take one last look at my disgusting, dirty, naked body before I turn for the shower.

Hot water cascades down my frame, washing away dirt and grime and blood. I haven't had the luxury of a shower since I was back at the House of Conrath. And, oh, how I have missed being clean.

When I exit the shower, I find clean clothes folded on the counter. Black slacks and a dark blue sweater. I smile in appreciation at Raheem's thoughtfulness and pull everything on.

Using just my fingers, I comb through my hair and let it hang loose.

"Are you hungry?" A crack in the bathroom door opens and Raheem's face appears.

A little smile pulls on my lips, and I nod.

A simple spread waits for us on the kitchen table when I walk out. Exotic cheeses and flat bread. Dehydrated fruits and nuts. Two plates and two glasses of water.

"Thank you," I say sincerely as I sit on one side when Raheem pulls my chair out for me. "For everything."

"You are a Royal," he says as he pushes the serving plate in my direction. "Some of us at the castle haven't forgotten that."

I shake my head as I gather food onto my plate. "It isn't just that. You always offer exactly everything that I need. I don't know how you always manage it, but you do."

And I look up just as I finish speaking, just in time to catch the flicker of pain that darts across his face.

Need.

Not long ago Raheem and I kissed, very passionately, and then had a discussion about what we were. He had pinned us exactly. Just need. Not love.

Need.

A fissure opens up in my chest, running right down the center of me.

I have to tell him.

I have to be honest.

But I want to throw up just thinking about it.

"I have to tell you something," I say. And it comes out as barely more than a whisper. My eyes have difficulty rising to meet his. And when they do, he's hardly paying attention, taking a bite out of his dinner. He has no idea what is coming.

"Cyrus lied to me," I say, suddenly not hungry in the least. And this does bring Raheem's eyes to mine. "He told me that the night I died, that Ian had left me. For good."

And a thought comes to me then. Raheem was in the room that night, as well. He saw everything that happened.

"Did you know?" I ask in a quiet voice.

A mix of emotions rolls over his face and his eyes drop away from mine.

"Please," I beg. "Tell me the truth."

He takes a sip of his water, stalling in answering. One beat. Two.

"You died, and Mr. Ward went ballistic," he finally says. "Two court members rushed into the room and started dragging him away. The entire time, Ian was yelling 'she did this because of you.' They took him away. The next day, when Cyrus was telling your House members that Ian had left, this time for good, I did not question it."

Something bites at the back of my eyes and I shake my

head. For the first time ever, I feel betrayed by Raheem. And it makes my stomach roll.

"Well, he didn't leave. And you certainly failed to tell me that it was him that bit me and ended my life. He's here," I say as I stand. I walk back toward the door. "He's down in the prison with me."

I open the door to reveal the guard who brought me here. "I'm ready to go back to my cell," I tell him.

"Alivia, I—"

"Thank you for everything you've done for me," I say through a thick throat as the guard begins chaining me back up. "I understand why you did what you did."

"Alivia, don't," he says as he takes a step toward me, but I walk out the door, dragging the guard behind me.

I get down five steps before I turn back to where Raheem stands in the doorway. "I forgive you," I say as my heart breaks just a little more. "Truly. I don't hold this against you."

I study his eyes and see in them that he doesn't believe me. Which is okay because I'm trying to decide if I really believe myself. I want to. But I've been manipulated and betrayed so many times.

So I turn around and continue walking down the stairs, chained like the prisoner that I am.

CHAPTER THREE

THE SUN TRIES TO BLAZE behind the dark gray clouds. Fat raindrops missile into the cell and splash to the floor, creating an enormous puddle on the stone. The pain is less severe than most days, but still I wish to claw my eyes from my skull just to end the burning and searing.

But slowly, the sun sets. Slowly, I am able to unwrap the sweater from around my eyes. Slowly, I take deep pulls once again, breathing in the moist and cold air. The sun fades away, but the rain does not cease.

I let out a sigh of relief as darkness engulfs me. Resting my back against a steel wall, I open my eyes and study the one opposite me.

For just a moment, I listen to the prisoners that surround me. Down four cells, the German man rustles for just a moment and then not thirty seconds later, begins snoring loudly. The Spanish man paces in his cell. The unknown silent one huffs as if they are doing pushups.

And Ian. I hear him breathe. Just on the other side of this wall. Slow. Thoughtful.

My heart aches.

I don't think my heart has stopped aching in years.

"Why does everyone lie, Ian?" I ask through the dark.

He doesn't answer me right away, but I hear his breathing change and know he's heard me.

"I feel like everyone has lied to me my entire life," I say as the weight on my chest grows heavier. "My mother lied by omission. By never telling me who my father was. Rath would never tell me anything about Henry. Cyrus said he was the one who killed me. Raheem let me believe you really did leave."

I let my head fall back against the wall with a dull *thunk*. "Maybe they don't so much as lie all the time, as they keep secrets."

"People just want to protect themselves," Ian finally responds. This voice is thick, muffled, as if he didn't really intend to speak out loud.

As I think back on every scenario, I find he's right. My mother was protecting herself. Rath was protecting his own heart from more pain at having lost his brother. Cyrus was protecting his small chance at winning my heart, and Raheem the exact same.

Who am I to judge? I've kept my own secrets. I still keep my secrets. And it is to protect myself.

"At some point, we're all going to be hurt by the lies and secrets that those we love keep from us," he says quietly. I hear him rub a hand over his face and then through his hair.

"Do you think you'll ever find out who your biological father is?" I ask.

He lets out a small sound of disgust. "Highly doubtful. The only way would be to ask my mom, and she's been dead for fifteen years."

"Would you ever want to know?" I ask as my brows furrow.

Ian doesn't respond right away. I can practically hear the gears turning in his head. Mulling it over, considering the consequences. "I honestly don't know," he finally says. "I loved my dad, the man who raised me. He and my mom were fire and ice, always bound to extinguish one another. They were no good together. And when I first found out, all I wanted to do was hunt down and kill the vampire who impregnated my mom."

He pauses for a long time, his breathing growing deeper, more ragged. "But now..."

Ian can't continue. And I understand it. Finally. He's come to see that not all vampires are what they seem by their name. The longer he is one, the more he's connecting the crooked and gray dots. The more he sees that he is a part of this picture.

"It's okay to be curious," I say as a sad little tug pulls at my heart.

Two more weeks. Fourteen days of sun. Fourteen days of burning. Days of starvation and dehydration. Sleepless days and nights.

I feel like death. And I have no doubt I look like it, too.

The German man is dragged away one day and doesn't return. Two women are brought into the prison. One cries almost constantly. The other doesn't say a word.

The rain continues to fall, and soon, the entire floor of my cell is covered in water. My skin is constantly pruned. My lungs vie for dry air to breathe, so I simply stop breathing more than once every few minutes.

Ian coughs from the next cell over, the first sound anyone has made in at least twelve hours.

"You okay?" I ask as I huddle on my flat, hard platform of a bed.

"Fine," he says. I hear him shuffle, turning on his own bed. I imagine him lying flat on his back, his hands behind his head, staring up at the ceiling.

I tuck my knees into my chest, my back pressed against the hard stone. My old human instincts tell me to shiver, that it's cold and wet, and I should be freezing. But this vampire body of mine doesn't feel anything.

"Can you tell me something, Liv?" Ian asks.

"What?"

He takes a few deep breaths, taking his time in

deciding how to ask his question. “Were you happy? Having the House and everything that came with it?”

I pick at a piece of fuzz on the hem of my sleeve. “I don’t know if happy is the right word,” I respond. “It’s hard to be happy when the King is always looming over your head. When Jasmine was making constant attacks on me. She and Micah are dead, by the way.”

Ian makes a surprised grunt, but doesn’t say anything.

“It’s kind of hard to be happy when your heart is broken,” I add quietly. But I need more truth. More honesty. Because I’m so, so tired of lies and secrets. “But in a way, I felt...completed, I guess. Running the House. I had a purpose. Before I moved to Silent Bend and found out about...everything, I just kind of, got by. I went through the motions of being a responsible adult, but I never did anything of worth. I just was.”

He’s quiet for a while, taking in what I’ve said.

“I never had a purpose until I found the House. I know you hate everything this system is and everything it stands for, but I did some great things while I ruled, Ian,” I say. “We were helping the town. We were protecting Silent Bend from this Snake army. I even got Markov to stop feeding on anyone in the borders.”

“That is quite the accomplishment,” Ian says with a little bit of a smile in his voice.

I feel one pull at my own mouth.

“Being dragged away from it was a lot harder than I

expected," I continue. "I know you hate them, but those vampires, they're my family. They're all I have."

Another long pause. "Most of them have been a part of Jasmine's broken House for a long time, and they followed the Kask's father before that. And I grew up hating them, because they were the same as what killed my mom and dad. So, I think when you accepted your birthright, it felt like you were welcoming their killer into your home. I couldn't separate the actions of one from the masses."

"That makes sense," I say with a nod. "And they're all far from perfect. They make mistakes. But so do humans. No one is perfect. Ever."

"No one is perfect," he whispers in an echo.

And as he says the words, I feel something in him change.

That hard edge softens.

FOR ANOTHER WEEK, WE ROT in prison. Another prisoner is brought down, an older sounding man who I swear sleeps all the time. Even if he is a vampire.

A letter is slipped under my cell door. I open it up to reveal handwriting that is difficult to read, as if English is not the first language they learned to write in.

I'm so sorry, my nofret. R

It's no question, R for Raheem.

I don't know what to respond back. Not that I could

respond. My feelings toward him are so incredibly complicated and twisted at the moment.

And time keeps passing.

So to pass the time, I catch Ian up on everything that has happened since he removed himself from my life. The tearing down of Jasmine's house. The arrival of the King. The games. The way we massively expanded. My descent into darkness. Rath's departure from the House of Conrath.

The plot to frame me.

Everything.

I leave out no small detail, because I have to get all of the secrets and lies out of me.

Including my involvement with Raheem.

"Do you love him?" Ian asks quietly. We've struck this weird balance of re-building friendship and keeping our past emotions and feelings removed. We're repairing and not laying out judgment.

It's not love, it's just...need. Raheem had said it, and while I'm not sure it was true for him, it was for me. "No," I answer. "I needed him. He was there, offering what I desperately craved at my weakest point. But I don't love him."

No matter how unfair it is.

"Do you still need him?"

Now that is a complicated question.

"Doesn't matter," I say, easing back from this circle of ease we've created between us. "I'm probably going to die soon, anyway. If they don't forget about me down here for forever."

"You're not going to die," he says. "They will see you have no reason to try and kill the King, all those Royals. Your House will come through."

"We'll see," I sigh.

TWO DAYS LATER, ANGRY VOICES descend the stairs, hurried and chaotic. I leap from my bed and walk over to the door. Steel screeches against steel and suddenly, Ian yells.

"The King's got a problem, and you're just the man to take care of it, I hear." I recognize that voice. Godrick. One of the Court members who came with Cyrus to Silent Bend.

"What are you talking about?" Ian demands. I hear him struggle as chains clang and a fist meets flesh.

"Got a vampire who needs putting down. One who's trying to run," Godrick's deep voice bellows, echoing off the walls. "You catch him, put him down, the King says he'll release you."

"Release..." Ian questions. Suddenly, he gives a hiss of pain. "Ah!"

"To keep you from running," Godrick says with a smile in his voice. "You don't return to the castle with a body in forty-eight hours, this little chip under your skin will detonate. A hundred wooden barbs shot straight into your heart."

"Ian!" I yell.

"It'll be fine!" he yells, and already, I hear his voice retreating. "I'll be back soon!"

And then, it's silent. He's gone.

CHAPTER FOUR

THERE ARE FORTY-EIGHT HOURS BEFORE something implanted into Ian will kill him. Within those forty-eight hours, there are twenty-four of them in the daylight. How is he supposed to use those hours? I can only hope they gave him some sun goggles.

I could sit here and drive myself mad with worry.

Or I could do something to distract myself.

"Tell me about yourself," I say, loudly enough to be heard. My voice echoes against the steel walls, being absorbed by the stone ones.

"Who are you talking to?" the Spanish man asks.

"Any of you," I say. I stand with my back against the wall. "All of you."

"Why do you care?" he responds. "We're all probably going to die, anyway."

"Death or not, I'm getting awfully tired of the silence," I say. "How about I start?"

He gives a little scoff, but doesn't protest.

"My name is Alivia Ryan," I begin. "I've only been Resurrected for about two months. I didn't know I was a Born until about nine months ago. I'm from the States. My father was Henry Conrath, my uncle Elijah. I've heard I'm a descendant of the third son."

"Conrath," a woman's voice perks up. The silent one who came in with the crier. "He was a House leader. Does that mean you are, too?"

I nod, even though she can't see me. "Yes. My uncle who ruled was killed quite some time ago. I just recently took over leadership."

"You're the most recent queen investigation," a deep voice rumbles—the silent man who hasn't made a peep since arriving. The accent is thick, African sounding.

"Yes," I say. "As you can guess, things didn't go so well."

"Someone really does want to take you down," the Spaniard says. "I think it's safe to say we all heard you telling your boyfriend everything. Somebody set you up bad. No wonder everyone thinks you did it."

"Yet you knew nothing about our world until a few months ago?" a new voice perks up. The crier.

"No," I say, shaking my head. I wish I could see the other prisoners. To read their faces and see what they really are thinking about what I am saying. "What are your names?"

"Horatio," the Spaniard offers right away. "From Spain."

"Luce," the quiet woman says. "And my sister Lina." The crier. "We're from Vancouver."

"My name is Obasi," the African says. "I am a child of all Africa. I fall under no House."

There's strength in Obasi's statement. Defiance. Fight.

"It's nice to finally speak to you all," I say, smiling to myself.

"Who do you think they dragged your boyfriend off to kill?" Horatio asks, a hint of amusement in his voice.

I shrug. "I'm sure the King has plenty of enemies he needs taken care of. It could be anyone."

"And what makes him so specifically qualified to take care of this?" Luce asks.

"He didn't know he was a Born, either," I say, debating how much of someone else's history I can disclose. But I'm tired of holding things at bay. And besides, Ian is going to be released soon. "Before he Resurrected, he was a hunter. He protected the town where my House is."

"Sounds like a complicated relationship," Luce says.

"You have no idea," I breathe out. A million miles of complicated strings attached. "Tell me, why are all of you here?"

It's a bold question, but one they asked of me. I hope

I've offered enough of my own secrets to gain some of theirs.

"My sister fell in love with the wrong man," Luce says. And there's a hint of an edge to her voice—resentment, anger. But protectiveness. "He is engaged to the House leader in the Pacific Northwest. When this leader found out what was going on, there was a confrontation. I couldn't just idly sit by."

"So, the House leader sent you here?" I ask in surprise.

Neither of them answers me straight away, and I can just imagine the looks between them. "Attempts on a Royal's life are never dealt with in a gentle manner," Luce finally says.

I am not sure what to say at first. Who is right and who is wrong in how this situation is being dealt with, I'm not entirely sure. "The heart does have a way of cutting in and making things messy." It's all I have to offer to the two of them.

The air is weighted, heavy. I can only imagine the tension that must exist between these sisters.

"I hope things work out for you both." I say it quietly. But I don't know that I have much hope. The brutality of the Court is so obvious, and I've not even gone through my own trial yet.

"What about you, Horatio?" I move on.

"I said something that offended a Court member," he says. "I think he put me in here just to get a backhanded laugh in."

"So, you should be released any time?" I respond.

"I should expect so," he says, and his tone implies he has nothing more to discuss about the situation.

Suddenly, feet sound on the stone steps, two sets of them, through the passageway and then stopping in front of my cell. A key grates in the lock, and a moment later, it slides open to reveal Trinity, a guard once again behind her.

"Holy shit," she breathes, her eyes going wide. She steps forward, placing her hands on my upper arms as she takes in my sad state. "Have they fed you at all since they brought you down here?"

I shake my head, even as my eyes search her over quickly. She seems in good shape. Clean clothes. No black veins of hunger.

"What's going on?" I ask, now searching her eyes for answers. "It's got to have been a month now. What's happening?"

"Christian and Markov are on their way here," she says. She sounds nervous. "They should arrive in two days and then your trial will start."

"They're coming here?" I ask in disbelief. "Does that mean they found evidence to prove me innocent?"

She shrugs, the look in her eyes telling me she's overwhelmed. She may be over forty-years-old Resurrected, but she's trapped in the body of a seventeen year old, and she's still that age in so many ways. "I don't know. The Court won't tell me much of anything."

"What *do* you know?" I demand. I take a step toward her. "Is everything okay in Silent Bend? Have there been any more attacks?"

She shakes her head. "I don't know!" she says defensively, acting nervous. "All I know is that things are finally going to move forward. Those two are on the way."

I nod my head, frustrated. "What about Ian? Have you heard anything about what's happening?"

"Just some radical type that the King didn't like," Trinity says as she sits on my platform bed. "But I did hear Cyrus is going to release him if he kills whoever it is."

So, maybe it is true, that they will let Ian go. Not just an empty promise.

I let out a slow breath. "So, what do you think? Are they going to convict me?"

Trinity shakes her head. "I don't know. I've been listening around the castle, but it's almost like they've forgotten about you. No one is saying anything about what happened."

"It feels like I've been forgotten," I say. I've already spent half of my life as a vampire in this prison.

"There is something," she says. "The third son wants to meet you."

My blood runs slow and cold at that. King Cyrus himself is a legend, a man most vampires are never likely to meet. Now I have. But almost as enigmatic as the King are his grandsons. Once there were seven of them, but they rose up against Cyrus, with his son. So the King killed most of those who rebelled, and gave the world to the two that did not.

I am a descendent of the third son. My claim to royalty.

"When?" I ask, my heart suddenly racing.

"At some point in the trial," she says. "I think you're about to meet a lot of very important people, Alivia."

"Time's up," the guard says, suddenly yanking the door open.

"Thank you," I say to her as I follow her toward the door. "Please, if you hear anything more, come tell me."

"I will if I can," she says, offering a sad smile before the door slides closed between us.

The footsteps retreat, and then it's just us prisoners once again.

"At least one of us is getting out of here soon," Horatio says. "Dead or alive."

CHAPTER FIVE

"IT'S TIME," A VOICE GROWLS from behind my prison door. It slides open, and two sets of hands grab me roughly. They drag me from my cell as a yelp leaps from my throat. I don't even have time to get my feet under me before they're hauling me across the stone floor, down the passageway.

"Good luck," Luce says quietly.

"I hope you survive," Obasi says.

Through hall after hall, stairways, across ballrooms and chambers, we circle and climb throughout the castle. I get to my feet and willingly follow behind them, but they drag me roughly and unnecessarily.

Finally, we stop in a hallway. It's grand and wide. Stone stretches all around us, rising up and up, wooden rafters spanning the air. And before us waits an enormous set of doors.

And X.

Her nose wrinkles and a disgust fills her face. "She reeks. You can't send her in like that."

A sharp breath intakes into my chest as a bucket of water is splashed over my head. I'm soaked in most places, my hair plastered to my forehead. I stand in a puddle on the cold floor.

X shakes her head, a cold look creeping into her eyes. "No," she says. "Not good enough. It's saturated into her clothes."

A large, rough hand suddenly grabs me from behind and instantly, my sweater is torn from my body. I don't even have time to react before another greedy hand shreds my pants.

And not a moment later, a second bucket of water is dumped over my head, drenching my body that is now only covered by my bra and panties.

"That's an improvement," X says, a cold smile on her lips as she looks at me. "Not so high and mighty now, are you, Lady Conrath?"

"Why so hostile, nameless chancellor?" I ask as I crook an eyebrow at her. I sound far more confident than I feel. I push my hair out of my eyes, running my fingers through it. "What did I ever do to you?"

"You tried to kill my King, of course," she says. Her smoky eyes look up at me from beneath long lashes. "Or have you forgotten?"

"Or perhaps because I didn't commit the crime," I say

as I wrap my arms around my middle.

I'm playing a tough game; I still have to be a leader. But I'm nearly naked and have no idea what to expect on the other side of that door.

"That remains to be determined," she says with another smile. She tosses me a thin, white sheath, which I pull over my wet body. She turns to the doors and pushes them open.

They reveal a great ballroom, one of dozens in the castle. The space opens wide, the ceiling high. Five black chandeliers hang above us, crystal dripping from them like dew drops. Great tapestries decorate the walls. A massive red rug dominates much of the floor.

And seated before me, in five great chairs, are a handful of familiar faces. Terror and shock saturate my bones.

Cyrus, seated in the middle, of course. He stares at me with dark, empty eyes.

To his left and right are two men I do not recognize. There's wisdom in their eyes, age.

But it is the last two faces that make the breath catch in my throat.

To the King's right is Lillian Summers.

To his left sits Elle Ward.

"What-" I begin to question.

But the King cuts me off.

"Alivia Ryan Conrath," he says in that booming, commanding voice. "You have been brought to *Roter*

Himmel, accused of treason, the murder of a Royal, and over a dozen Born. And the attempted murder of your King. How do you plead?"

It takes me a moment to process everything. The jurors. The accusations. "Not...not guilty."

A displeased but amused smile tugs at Cyrus' lips as his eyes darken further. "Lady Conrath, your trial will begin come daybreak when your House representatives arrive. Until that point, you will be kept in solitary with a constant guard."

He gives a dismissive wave of the hand, and the guard has just grabbed me when a heavy set of boots sound down the hallway. I turn just in time to see Ian round the hallway and approach.

His eyes widen when he takes me in, drenched and starved, his lips pressing into a thin line.

And I take him in, laying eyes on him for the first time in two months.

He's changed. His face is covered with a thick beard, his hair grown long enough for him to pull it back into a short tail at the nape of his neck. The youthful, handsome face I was once so familiar with is nearly unrecognizable with the hard lines that take over everything.

In his left hand, he holds a dismembered head by the hair.

The moment Ian's eyes slide from mine to take in the rest of the people behind him, I watch as if in slow motion, the change in his expression. The way his mouth opens in anger, his eyes as they widen in horror. The muscles of his body as they tense and flex as he darts forward.

"Elle!" he bellows as he races toward her.

Two guards rush Ian from either side, colliding with a great smack that nearly sends the three of them to the floor. "What is she doing here?" Ian bellows like a madman. "If you touched her-"

"Your dear sister has not been harmed," Cyrus cuts him off with an amused smile and commanding in his voice. "She has merely been brought here to serve as one of Alivia's judges. I would be very careful if I were you, Mr. Ward."

"Ian, don't," Elle says as she shakes her head. "I'm okay. Please. Just cooperate."

His eyes glow, so bright and red as he frantically searches his sister for signs of harm. But there aren't any. Just as the King said.

Slowly, I hear his heart calm, the breaths come a little slower. He swallows, blinking three times as he continues to search her. Her eyes plead for him to calm down, to not get himself into trouble.

So he does. Ian straightens, lifting his chin high. And slowly, the guards let him go. Ian doesn't bolt. Doesn't lunge.

He tosses the head he's holding so it lands just at the King's feet. "She was headed toward the mountains," he says, his eyes flicking between Cyrus and me. "Didn't take long to catch her."

Cyrus sneers down at the dismembered head. "Well done. We had a deal. You're free to go back to the swamp you call home. Unless you're interested in staying at Court? I could use a man with your...skills."

The disgust on Ian's face is obvious, the hatred in his eyes darkening by the moment. "Pass," he says through clenched teeth. "What are you going to do with Alivia?"

"Oh, your former plaything that you abandoned?" Cyrus says with a smirk. He leans forward, resting a forearm on his knee. Ian's jaw tightens in anger.

"Don't," I whisper to him, even though everyone in the room can hear it. "Just let it go, Ian."

"Yes, just let it go, Ian," Cyrus says, enjoying the torture he's putting the man through. "As you already did. Just let her go. Because her trial will begin come daybreak, and it doesn't look good."

Ian lets out a harsh breath through his nose, staring down the King, before turning to me. He takes five steps. "You okay?" he asks, the concern growing in his eyes.

"I'm fine," I say.

He stares at me hard, not believing what I'm saying. But finally, he turns back to the judges. "I'll leave," Ian says. "But not until after the trial is over. I need to make sure Alivia and my sister make it safely back to Silent Bend."

Cyrus chuckles and stands. He kicks the head out of his path, sending it rolling across the ballroom, flicking blood everywhere. He claps his hands together, rubbing his palms. "Ah, so I guess now we know what type you are. The brash hero who must protect everyone. What a cliché."

I hear it, the intake of breath Ian takes, about to say something he shouldn't to the King. My hand darts out, clamping down hard on Ian's forearm over his jacket. He gets the warning message, because he doesn't say a word.

Cyrus lets out a laugh, four short bursts of gleeful spite. He turns away from us, and the two guards grab me. I don't fight them, and Ian watches me, ready to spring, so I try to convey the message of *it's okay* through my eyes.

The guards don't have to force me as we turn and head out of the enormous room. Ian's footsteps follow just behind.

And just as we're ten feet through the doorway, Raheem rounds the corner.

His eyes grow wide and his expression pales. Not once do his eyes leave my face as he rushes forward. These guards must not know of Raheem's betrayal because they do not stop him when he reaches forward and takes my chained hands in his.

"Are you alright?" he asks, his eyes searching me over. "Are they beginning?"

And I feel heat clawing up my neck, spreading to my cheeks. My eyes dart to Ian, and sure enough, he's staring, a hard expression in his eyes.

"I'm fine," I say, unable to look him in the eye. "And they're beginning at daybreak when Christian and Markov arrive."

Finally, Raheem seems to catch on that we have an audience. His eyes dart to Ian. But he doesn't back down, doesn't seem embarrassed. But his eyes do harden. "Mr. Ward," he says. "I see you've been released from prison."

"Yep," Ian responds. His voice is tight. He crosses his arms over his chest, revealing the stake in his hand, exposing the long blade dangling from his hip.

"I assume you will be staying for the trial?" Raheem asks as he finally lets my hands go.

I groan. Romantic drama is the last thing I want right now. I step forward, dragging the guards behind me.

I don't wait for them to react. Don't turn around to see their heated stares.

Suddenly, isolation sounds like heaven.

CHAPTER SIX

THE ROOM THEY MOVE ME to is a massive improvement over the cell.

A simple double-sized bed sits in the middle of the small room. A dresser is on one wall. A mirror on another. A small bathroom. And then there's a closet with a few simple items of black clothing.

But it's heaven compared to the steel and stone walls I've been staring at for the last month.

The very first thing I do is shower. X was cruel, but right. I do smell awful. The last shower I got was the one I took in Raheem's quarters weeks ago. The hot water cascades down over me, rinsing off the filth and time.

When I'm done, I braid my hair, which has gotten so long, over my shoulder and pull on the clothes.

A knock sounds on the door and a moment later, a woman opens the door. My throat instantly burns.

She's human.

She's barely closed the door behind her, saying something with a heavy Austrian accent, before I'm across the room and my fangs sink into her neck.

The human woman goes instantly still, her head lolling to the side, exposing easier access. My fingers dig hard into her flesh, holding her upright, as my fangs sink in deeper. I take long pulls, drawing from her body what I've been craving for over a month now. Fresh blood.

But my age is showing. Just last month, I would have easily kept sucking until I drained her dry, but as the burn in my throat and belly begins to be extinguished, my thoughts clear. I release her after just a few deep pulls.

"Thank you," I say, wiping the back of my hand across my mouth. And it's the first time it's come away clean.

"*Bitte*," she says in German, offering me a pleasant smile. She turns to the door and knocks three times. A guard opens the door and lets the woman out.

I collapse into the bed, feeling both satisfied and disgusted with myself. I hadn't realized how badly I needed something fresh to drink. So much better than the bagged stuff.

And maybe it's finally getting to drink. Maybe it's finally knowing that something is going to happen. I claw my way up to the pillow and tuck myself into the blankets. Maybe it's having a real bed once again, but finally, I sleep for the first time in a month.

• • •

I'M WOKEN BY THE SOUND of talking outside the door to my room. I sit up in the dark and push a few loose strands of hair out of my face, just as the door is pushed open.

"Markov," I call in delight. I'm out of the bed in a blink and my arms wrap around his neck. "Christian." He gains a hug, as well.

"Told you they wouldn't just a let a Royal rot in a prison cell," Christian says with a smirk in Markov's direction.

"Actually," I correct him as we walk into the room and I settle back onto the bed. "I've only just been moved from the prison a few hours ago. I've been down there all this time."

Markov fixes Christian with a cold glare. "She may be a Royal, but she was removed as a prisoner. Are you well, my queen?"

The softness in his voice makes my heart swell. A kind word. A hint of loyalty. "I'm okay," I say, offering him an appreciative smile. "Even better now that you two are here. I guess three. Lillian is here, too."

Markov's eyes flash red for a moment, a look of disgust and frustration upon his face. Their expressions tell me they knew she was here. "She was your first ally, yet first to doubt you," Markov says, anger in his voice. "Did you ever see this coming?"

"No," I respond honestly. "I thought she was my friend. I thought—"

"She is your friend," Christian says. "That's why she's so hurt. The evidence does look pretty damn bad."

"Did you two find anything to prove that I'm being set up?" Suddenly, my voice is desperate.

Markov takes my hand in his, patting it between his two wrinkled and aged ones. "King Cyrus has mandated that we are not allowed to tell you anything before the trial. But I do believe we have a good chance of exonerating you."

There's enough doubt in his voice to make my heart race.

"Our case kind of all hinges on one important key, and it hasn't exactly been secured yet."

"That's enough," Markov hushes Christian. "You're a fool if you think Cyrus isn't listening to every word."

Christian takes two fingers and zips them over his lips, giving Markov an annoyed glare.

"How long until daybreak?" I ask as they stand to leave.

"About an hour," Markov responds. He smooth's his hands over my shoulders, clearing away the wrinkles in my clothes. "I'm sure they will come for you soon. Do not be intimidated by their numbers. You have loyalty at your side, people who know you did not commit this heinous crime."

"Chin up, princess," Christian says as he opens the door. "See you on the stand."

CHAPTER SEVEN

THEY DO INDEED COME TO get me in exactly one hour. The same two guards chain my wrists and ankles. I'm pretty sure it's all a mental game because surely, I could break them with just a few good yanks. But it would be foolish to fight them. I'm sure either of them would yank my heart from my chest without hesitation if I struggled.

Up two floors and down a long hall. It opens up to reveal a colossal room. A huge, massive table is set up, set in the shape of a square. The room is empty except for a few guards stationed at each of the entrances.

"Here," the female guard says, sitting me in a chair in the middle of one of the square's legs. She un-cuffs my bonds. "Don't try anything. You'll be staked before you can move a meter."

I glance back at her. Her fangs are extended, her eyes

glowing red with black veins on her face. And in her hands, she holds a crossbow with a wooden stake set and ready.

"Deal," I say.

The sound of feet on stone draws my eyes to the hallway once more, and a flock of bodies begins crowding into the room.

Godrick, Judith, Serge, and Raheem. A dozen other faces I do not recognize. Then Christian and Markov. A moment later, Ian. A few others. And finally, the judges. Lillian, who can't seem to quite look me in the eye. Elle, who is always unreadable. The two men I do not know. And finally, last of all, Cyrus.

"Welcome everyone," he says with false cheerfulness as everyone fills in around the table. But no one is allowed to sit beside me. The judges sit directly across, facing me, and everyone else fills in on the sides to my left or right. "Thank you, so much, for being here and being witness to this rare occurrence of treason. Why, the last time someone tried to kill me, the entire House of Greenland had to be executed!" He laughs at this, as if truly enjoying the replay going on in his head.

Cyrus stands at the head of the table, his fingertips resting on the wooden surface. "The trial will take time. We must be certain that we have all the pieces, that those who believe they have something of value to add have said their piece. So today, we only embark on the first leg of this voyage. Alivia—Lady Conrath—will give her statement. Her defense. She will answer the questions of the judges. But first," he says as he claps his hands. Suddenly, the room is filled with servants carrying dishes. "We eat."

The tables are stocked quickly. Gleaming metal dishes are placed before everyone, except me. Smells of roast and vegetables and bread float into the air and my stomach growls fiercely.

Plates are set before everyone and they do not hesitate in dishing up.

My mouth waters at the scent of everything. It's been so long since I ate a proper meal. When looking at myself in the mirror earlier, I guessed I've lost at least fifteen pounds, fifteen that I didn't really have to lose in the first place.

Vampires have to eat, just as humans do. But starvation won't kill us.

"I suppose," Cyrus says as he butters a roll, "since you are yet an infant in our world, and this is your first visit to Court, introductions should be made." He indicates the vampire to his right. "This is my grandson, Malachi, or as he is commonly referred to, the seventh son. And this," he indicates the other, "is Dorian, the third son. Of whom you are a descendent."

"I'd say it's nice to meet you," I say, bowing my head, "but under these extreme circumstances, I don't think I'm leaving the best impression."

"She's a Conrath, alright," Dorian says, a small smile

crooking his lips. “Sounds just like Elijah; looks just like her father.”

“No one has doubted her being a Conrath,” Markov speaks up. “Very few have questioned her birthright.”

“Royal lineage and rights or not,” a woman from the crowd says. “Treason is treason.”

I can barely concentrate on the conversation being had. I’m so hungry. My eyes dart around the table, drooling over those sautéed mushrooms. Dying for a taste of that buttered asparagus.

Suddenly, Ian stands and stalks over to me. To my great relief, he has a plate in his hand, filled with different foods. He sets it down in front of me.

“And who gave you permission to do so?” X demands, practically spitting fire.

I don’t wait for someone to rip the plate away; I’m digging in with my hands, ravenous.

“You expect her to defend herself when she can barely think straight from starvation?” Ian manages to defend me in a calm manor. “You let her rot with nothing for a month and then expect her to perform in front of a jury? Carefully, your royalnesses. You’re starting to look like you don’t want this to be fair, at all.”

“You will-”

“Now, now,” Dorian interrupts X. “This man has been cleared of any crime, released from prison. His presence here makes him a guest. Perhaps we will treat him as one.”

At once, she gains her composure back, throwing her hair over her shoulder, her eyes dropping to the table in silence. She may be the King's chancellor, but she was just put in her place.

"Before we begin," Cyrus moves on, "I must warn you all. Lady Conrath here is quite the actress. She, for some time during my visit to the States, made me believe she truly was Sevan, our beloved queen, returned to me after so long. While in the shadows, she was spending some very intimate time with our most decorated spy. I had no idea for some time. She hid her true feelings well. So please, let us keep that in mind as she tells us her tales."

I feel the eyes burn into me, see them shift to Raheem. Hear the intake of breath and the mutterings. I'm tempted to look at him, but I just can't.

"It's true," I say as I wipe my mouth with a napkin. "Raheem and I have...had feelings for each other. And it's true that I toyed with Cyrus. I was suffering from a broken heart, and I needed to hurt someone in return." My voice drops and my eyes fall from the crowd momentarily. "And, I think in the end I hurt two..." I shake my head, feeling sick over myself. "Three people."

I swallow hard, squaring my shoulders. My messed up love life is not the reason we are here. I need to focus. "But the point is that, having lost everything so quickly, having everything ripped away, has made me realize I am just one being and that control is a relative thing. It has made me realize that I own nothing but the truth."

The chair scrapes against the stone floor as I stand, pushing it back from the table. The chains that prove me prisoner clang against the table, sounding through the quiet room. "My father had a reputation. I'm not going to pretend otherwise. I know almost nothing about him, know nothing of his past, really, other than that he is a descendant of Dorian. But something in his past happened that made him turn his back on the monarchy and our system. You all have been around long enough, I'm sure you know what I am oblivious to."

I search their eyes at this statement. And see it there. They do know. Cyrus. Dorian. X. Probably others. They know so much more about Henry Conrath than I.

It's not fair.

I'm a girl who never knew her father.

"When my uncle was killed in 1875, leadership of the House of Silent Bend should have fallen to Henry's shoulders. But he refused. So the house fell into shame. Disgrace."

I swallow, shame and regret crawling up my throat.

Somehow, Rath plays into all of this. How old he is, I have no idea, but I'm sure he's seen so much. Advised my father, stood at his side.

And now, I've chased him away.

"I was born to a single mother twenty-three years ago," I say. At the memories of her, of our simple life, my lip threatens to quiver for a moment. But my vampire body has far more control than that. "I lived in Colorado.

For those not familiar with the United States, that's most of the way across the country from Silent Bend. My mother always told me that we were strong women, that we could do anything without a man. That my father wasn't real, and that we were all each other needed."

This does prick emotion at the back of my eyes. Because she taught me to be strong. But she was also wrong. I needed my father, and I never even knew it until I found him, only it was too late. He was already dead.

"I never even knew his name," I say quietly. The room around me is dead silent. They each hold onto my story with baited breath. "Not until a will showed up in my mailbox and I got a call from his attorney the next day saying I was his heir.

"I showed up at his house, and his staff wouldn't even look me in the eye," I say. "They seemed to be afraid of me, and I didn't understand why. I started talking to people in town, and they seemed to hate me when they found out who my father was."

I take a deep breath. This is emotionally draining, and I'm only at the very beginning. "I was attacked by a Bitten the very first day I left my house," I continue the tale. "I didn't understand what was happening. Why someone would bite me. Why I couldn't move or scream. I didn't believe any of this was real."

Oh, to go back to that day. To not have left my house. To have just gone back to Colorado after two days in Mississippi. How different my life would be right now.

I look over at Ian because I can't tell the rest of this story without involving him. Everything changed that night he intended to kill me.

"Ian knew everything," I say as I hold his eyes. And he stares deeply back at me. There it all is, there in his eyes. So much history in such a short amount of time. "He saved me from the Bitten, but knew it should have been too late for me. He was going to kill me. So I didn't become one of them."

"That doesn't prove anything," one of the Court members pipes up, the first word spoken from one of them yet.

"She was terrified!" Ian yells back in my defense. "She really thought she was dead. She didn't know anything!"

"Hold your tongue, Mr. Ward!" Malachi bellows from the head of the table. "This is not the day for witnesses. You will refrain from speaking or you will be thrown out of this deposition. That goes for you, as well." He spits this at the man of the Court who interrupted.

With everyone quiet, Malachi nods his head for me to continue.

And so, I do. With how I hid at Ian's house right after that because he and Rath were afraid Jasmine would come after me and try to sway me with only partial truths. How I confronted Jasmine, took control of my own fate.

How she killed Ian, and how I vowed to take the House from her.

Every move I made to gain my House members' loyalty. All the games I had to play with Jasmine.

The attacks that happened at her Broken House. All the people who went missing. How the town turned against me once more, just as I was gaining their trust.

As I tell it, the picture I was a part of becomes darker and darker. More sinister.

More gray.

"And then the King arrived," I say. "Just one day later, I died, and Resurrected. And, yes, I toyed with the King. Yes, I played the political games. Survived the King's own. Grew my House. And some of them might think I did this," I say as I meet Lillian's eyes. I'm hopeful when I see doubt there. Maybe she isn't as sure as I once feared. "But my House is my family. And I would never turn on my kind. Because I didn't know it then, but before I found my birthright, I was simply floating through life without a purpose. This is my calling, my home. I would never turn against my fellow Born, much less my King."

I bow my head then, letting my eyes slide closed.

It's true. The concept of a King is so foreign to my very normal upbringing in a land that has never had a king on its soil. But I stand before one now. He may be a sadistic man. He may have had far too much time on this earth. But I would never kill him.

The room is silent for a long time as I remain with my head bowed. I listen hard, hoping to hear breath of relief, they having been convinced of my innocence. But all I hear is silence.

Until a slow, loud clap sounds. Twice. Four times. Five. I look up.

"What a story," Cyrus breathes out. "My, my. She is quite compelling, is she not? Even I am not sure what the truth is. Did Alivia commit treason in the dark? Did she build an army behind the veil of the poor, fatherless child? Or has she been framed by someone so clever that we have never yet seen someone so invisible?"

He asks questions, but everyone at this table is intelligent enough to know better than to answer.

"Members of the jury," he says turning to them. "I want you to carefully consider the tale this woman has told. I want you to think about the personal experiences you have had with her." He looks at both Lillian and Elle. "And I want you to consider how bloodlines affect the genetic makeup of one's desires." Directed to Dorian and Malachi. "The trial will resume in two days."

The guards step up and grab hold of my arms. My eyes flit around the room. Elle. Lillian. Raheem and Ian both look worried, constantly wondering if this will be the last time they will see me alive. But they are each helpless to do anything at this point.

So that they will not fight, so that they will not endanger themselves, I follow behind the guards without a word.

They lead me once again on a path I will never be able

to retrace. Down stone steps, through passageways. Across grand, empty rooms.

Down and down, up, snaking back and forth.

The world feels darker, and a sinking feeling settles into my chest as we descend a set of stairs. I know I'm far from the prison. Far from the room I rested in just hours ago. And a black set of doors looms at the end of the hall we proceed down.

Music dances in my ears as we get closer. Pumping and loud. It shakes the floor. Vibrates the stones. The kind you'd hear at a club, but all the singing is in German, I think.

"What..." I begin to ask, but I'm so confused that I do not have words to say what I'm trying to put together.

"King's orders," one of the guards says, looking back at me with an amused sneer. "You toyed with his heart, now he's making you a toy of the Court."

We reach the door and the woman pulls it open, letting out a blast of the overwhelming music.

The scent of alcohol and drugs and bodies is overpowering. Heavy perfume hangs in the air, sickeningly sweet. There's a long hallway, the walls painted black with flecks of glitter mixed into the dark coats the walls. My guards lead me down the hall and it opens up into a room. A single, regal, high-backed chair sits in the middle of the room. Blood red in color. Purple curtains hang all around. Black lights glow from just behind them.

Just before the chair, a few feet away, is a floor-to-ceiling steel pole.

"What the hell is going on?" I demand as the guards shove me to one side of the room, where a hand appears from behind the curtains, holding it back for us to pass into yet another hallway.

A man wearing only a leopard-print thong smiles sadly at me as he watches us pass by. My heart leaps into my throat, threatening to choke me. For the first time, I tug at my bonds. I slow my steps.

But the guards force me forward. And I see two girls toward the end of the hall. They wear little more than lingerie. They stare, their eyes running up and down me. A little red glow ignites in one of their eyes.

A man comes next, wearing only a pair of tight briefs. And then, my throat burns when the next one I walk past is human. But there is no fear in her eyes.

The hallway suddenly opens up into what appears to be a huge dressing room. A wall of mirrors and dim lights dominate one side, chairs dotting along the counter beneath the mirror. Make up and wigs and all kinds of fake and lustful things line it.

And there are dozens of men and women in here, Born and human alike. Changing, naked, nearly naked in just bras and underwear. Others strutting around like their nakedness doesn't mean anything at all.

"Is this her?"

A clear voice suddenly jerks me from my wonder and

disgust. I look to the side to see a woman standing there, looking me up and down. She's young, no more than twenty. Long, dark hair falls midway down her back in soft, perfect curls. Meticulous, minimalistic makeup dots her creamy-colored face.

She wears a simple black dress that stretches to the floor, though exposing all of her cleavage.

"This is her," the guard says, tightening his grip on my arm. Were I human, I'd be deeply bruised. "You have the King's orders, I presume?"

She cocks an eyebrow at me, a small smile on her lips. "He was very specific. She must have really pissed him off."

The guard chuckles and shoves me forward, just as the female guard jabs something into my back, right above my heart. I hiss in pain, pulling away from them.

"You'll do as Madame says for the next two days," the male one says. "Or the implant will explode, as will your heart. He's got cameras everywhere in the club, so don't try anything clever."

He pushes me from behind with enough strength to send me to my knees. I barely catch myself from falling on my face since my hands are chained together.

"You've got the controller," the female guard says. "If she steps out of line, the King says not to hesitate in setting it off."

"I understand," the woman they refer to as Madame says. "I'll take it from here."

I look back to see the male guard giving me a smirk before they both turn to leave.

"Stand up," Madame says. "Our clients here will know you're a Royal, seeing you on the ground like this could go from one extreme to another."

Slowly, I pick myself up from off the polished marble floor. I'm still looking around, taking it all in.

There's a woman, completely naked, talking to another woman while she preps herself in the mirror. She laughs, acting as if it's no big deal that her breasts are out in the open, for all to see, or that her voluptuous back end is exposed.

Yet none of these people seem bothered by the nudity. They don't steal glances, don't look at all. As if they're completely desensitized.

"I'm sure you can guess what this place is," Madame says, dragging my attention back to her. It's then that I realize her accent is American. "We dance here, for men or women. Some of the clients are here for more...extreme forms of pleasure, blood or skin. I'm in charge here. I hire the employees, schedule appointments. Make sure everyone is doing their job. And the King has sent you here, to me, for the next two days."

"I don't understand," I say as sweat prickles along my skin.

"Oh, I think you do," Madame says as a flat smile pulls on her red lips.

"Please," I say. Because I think I do, too, but I just can't quite accept it. "Spell it out for me."

"Okay," she says as she starts walking around me in a circle. "King Cyrus can hold a grudge like you wouldn't believe. For being thousands of years old, his memory is impeccable. He forgets nothing. And fresh on his memory, is how you misled him. How you made him believe."

She reaches out and gathers a handful of my shirt. She gives it a great yank and rips it clean from my skin. As startled as I am, the expression on her face is calm. As if she is simply doing her job. She gains no pleasure or sadness from her actions.

"You thought it a good idea to play with the King, and now he is going to turn you into the Court's favorite new, shiny toy," she says. Once again, she rips my clothing from my body, leaving me in only a dirty bra and underwear and simple flats.

I'm exposed, left defenseless in every way.

"You played with the King, and now he is going to whore you out to his descendants."

CHAPTER EIGHT

"SHOWER, AND THEN NATALIA WILL help you do your hair and makeup," Madame says as she walks with me to the far end of the dressing room. She does indeed stop at a shower. But there's no door, no curtain. "And don't worry about being a prude. No one back here cares about your body."

Embarrassment spikes in my blood as I look around once again. No one is paying me any mind, they're all busy prepping themselves, or talking, or sitting and reading as they wait to go on stage, I assume.

"Hurry up," Madame says impatiently. "I really don't have all day."

I want to fight. To knock her on her back and bolt. But there's still the dull ache in my back where the guard implanted the explosive. If I make a wrong move, she'll detonate my heart, and I'll be dead for good this time.

So, I turn my back to her and strip out of my underthings, hiding my father's necklace in my clothes.

Barely warm water washes over me. But as I scrub my skin, wash my hair, I only feel dirtier, exposed to this disgusting place. I keep my back turned to the room, cleaning myself as quickly as I can. The minute all of the suds wash off of my body, I shut the water off.

"See, that wasn't so hard, was it?" Madame walks back over, extending a towel out to me. I quickly wrap it around myself. "This way."

She leads me to the wall of mirrors and instructs me to sit on one of the stained, padded stools. "Natalia," Madame yells down the row.

Natalia is obviously a man. But he's painted as a beautiful woman. Wears an overly sexual teddy. "Oh, everyone out there is going to love her," Natalia says when she reaches me, raising perfect eyebrows at my dripping wet appearance. "She's gorgeous."

"She's to be the star of the show tonight, so make her shine," Madame says with a smile as she lays a hand on Natalia's arm before walking away.

"It's what I do best," she says with a bright smile.

She starts brushing through my wet hair, adding in a little bit of product. She produces a blow dryer and soon my hair is being tugged and pulled and blown every direction.

"So, you're a Royal, I hear," she says when she's finally done drying. She moves on to a curling iron. "Is it true?"

I bite my lower lip, looking up at her heavily made up eyes. I'm terrified to be here. I want to get this over as quickly as possible. Conversation wasn't expected. Finally, I nod.

"So, are you a descendent of Dorian or Malachi?" she asks as she winds my hair around the hot iron. "Because, girl, around here, it seems to matter more and more these days. I swear, someday Malachi's posterity will just wipe out those of Dorian, except their numbers are so large, they could never actually stand a chance if it ever came to battle."

Natalia goes on and on, not actually expecting any response from me. And, I find she's actually fascinating to listen to. She shares far more information than I bet she's supposed to.

I learn that all the dancers here are descendants of the exiled grandsons. They're Born, but have never had any claim to royalty. They're the only exiled allowed in *Roter Himmel*. They make up about two-thirds of the employees of *Klub Blut und Lüste*, which I assume is the name of this club. Humans make up the other third.

There's some kind of hard feelings between the Born and the human dancers. The clients who come to the club often prefer the humans because they're allowed to feed on them while they engage in...activities. But they do have a large turnover rate. Not everyone who visits the club has good control.

If the humans are turned, they're killed the minute they wake up as a Bitten.

Less pay as a Born stripper, but better job security.

Natalia never once stops talking as she moves from my hair to my makeup. And she takes her time. Foundation. Contouring. Heavy, heavy eye makeup. Lipstick.

I watch myself in the mirror as she transforms my face. I'm radiant. Glowing in the dim light. In some ways, I feel beautiful. But that face looking back at me, it isn't me. I'm buried under five pounds of cake.

And it makes me feel better about this new prison I've been sent to. It's not me that's going to be forced to do whatever they have planned for me. I'm buried under the mask. Hidden deep inside until this passes over.

"Look at you!" Natalia coos as she finishes with me. "They are going to love you tonight!"

She sets the last of her tools on the table and lets me take it in one last time.

"Thank you," I say through a thick throat, trying to smile. "You did a wonderful job."

"It's what I do best," she repeats once again, flashing that brilliant smile. Looking around, she spots Madame and signals her over.

"Nice work, as always, Natalia," she offers with an approving look-over. "I think Joanne needs you next."

I'm almost sad when Natalia flitters away to whore up the next victim. She kept my mind off of what was coming up next.

"This is your costume for tonight," Madame says, holding out something on a hanger. "Get dressed and then we'll give you some pointers."

I take the hanger from her, but I'm not even sure how to put this thing on. Lace and straps dangle all over the place.

"Please hurry up," Madame says as she walks over to a man, who's fully dressed, and takes a black box he offers.

I stand and make my way to the darkest corner of the dressing room. Once again turning my back to everyone, I attempt to figure out the contraption.

It's not quite as intimidating as I thought at first. A deep red lacy bra that actually hides nothing has little crisscrossing straps that stretch down my sides, attaching to the panties, leaving my stomach and back exposed. The panties are lacy, as well, and ride up my crack, exposing most of my butt.

A pair of black heels, five inches tall, accompany the number. I slip them on and am surprised when they're not as impossible to walk in as I expected.

"Yes, you'll do nicely," Madame says in approval as I walk back over to her. "Although, those certainly mar the appeal a bit."

I cover my stomach with my hands, embarrassed. The two red scars that stretch up from my panty line stand out in bright contrast to my pale skin.

"No matter, their focus isn't going to be on them," she

says, setting the black box on a chair and opening it. "But on this."

From the box, she produces a crown.

My crown.

The golden one with the raven symbol affixed in the center of it. Upon closer observation, I see it is not my actual crown. But it's a nearly perfect replica.

So not only are they going to get a rise out of my station, Cyrus has chosen to publicly shame my entire family and House.

"Don't fight it my dear," Madame says, lifting the crown and placing it on my head. "As I said, the King was very specific about his orders."

"I will serve my penance," I say with a false smile.

"That's a good girl," she says as she leads me back to one corner of the changing room. She pulls back a curtain and yells for someone, speaking in German. Two girls follow us in. We enter into a smaller room, lit only with a black light. And standing in the center of the room is a pole.

Madame speaks to them again in German, fast and quick. I wonder where she is from. When she speaks English, her accent is perfectly American, but she seems to speak German with perfect ease.

"Watch them closely," Madame says, turning to me. "They will show you some basics. You'll need all this for tonight."

I can't believe I'm here, watching these two girls grind

and swing around this pole. I can't believe I'm being forced into this. I can't believe how quickly life can change.

But there is something hypnotic about it all. Something primal. Carnal.

Even I can't seem to look away from their movements, and I've never been attracted to a woman.

Klub Blut und Lüste. So fitting.

"Now, you," Madame says, waving her hand for me to take the pole. "I need to be sure you aren't going to go out on stage and just awkwardly hump the pole."

I'm a little offended, but I can't say she's wrong.

I've never done this before.

The girls' movements are still fresh in my mind, so I do my best to repeat them. Sliding up and down, swinging with one leg wrapped around it. I feel so exposed and open, like everything I'm wearing is going to fall apart and leave me naked and bare.

"It's not perfect, but it'll do," Madame says. She turns to the girls again and says something in German. They exit the room.

"You'll go on in just a few minutes. The first stage of all of this is just a dance," she explains. She's so calm and collected about it all. I wonder how much of her immortal life has been spent here in the basement of the castle, managing these girls and boys. "The clients aren't allowed to touch the stage dancers. Any money they might offer will be split between the employees. You'll be informed about stage two shortly."

My heart starts racing as I hear the thumping song begin to wind down. Madame leads me out, back into the dressing room, to another curtained wall, which she pulls back to reveal a hallway.

Down we go, but not very far. The dark hall lightens, and I hear many, many bodies on the other side of a curtain.

Suddenly, two women step through it, barely giving us a side-glance before they walk by.

A voice booms through a speaker system. I don't understand the words, but I certainly recognize when they announce "Lady Conrath."

"That's you," Madame says. Suddenly, her hands are on my back, and she shoves me through the curtain.

Lights temporarily blind me. Blue and purple laser lights dance around the space. Slowly, more and more of the scene processes through my brain.

Black walls. Dimly glowing lights set along them. The stage I stand on has lights along the edge of it. And down below, there are so many chairs. Booths, tables. A bar lines the back of the big room.

And filling every one of the chairs, is a body.

Men. Women.

Each of them staring at me with lustful eyes.

I process all of this in two seconds. And then they go crazy. Cheering. Hollering. Cat-calls. They go ballistic over my crown. Over the little amount of clothing I wear, and the harsh lights that expose all of me.

A deep beat starts and the tempo of the music picks up. I allow myself to stand there, gaping, for just one second, before a voice hisses from behind me. "Do it, or I'll have to kill you." Madame.

So, my eyes still focused on the crowd, I grab the pole with one hand. And I've never been stripped down, so exposed, literally and figuratively. I swing my body around the pole, sliding down, keeping it tight between my thighs.

I was a queen just weeks ago.

I was a ruler.

I led a house of over twenty.

And now, I've fallen.

I've been reduced to a plaything, using my body for the entertainment of others.

My pride got the best of me. It was my downfall. Thinking I could run with the oldest of them.

I may be a House leader, but I still know so little.

I must remember that.

The music thumps, loud and sexual. I twirl. I grind. I bend.

Money flies in my direction. The hollers do not cease. Words are shouted at me, thankfully in German, so I do not understand the disgusting things they are surely yelling at me.

I zone them all out. I pretend they are not here. I let my body take over, setting myself on autopilot.

But this song feels endless.

Never ceasing.

My vampire brain keeps track of the seconds that lead into minutes. Five go by. Surely, the song must end. But then it stretches on to ten minutes. And finally at fifteen, the music begins to wind down.

The announcer comes back on, again speaking words I do not understand. And as the song ends, Madame suddenly steps from the curtain. She takes my hand in hers, holding it high in the air. She says something I do not understand, and even more money is thrown towards us.

I put on a fake smile because as they said, the King has cameras all over this place. I need to be a good little prisoner.

One last statement from Madame and then she turns us, and back into the hallway we go.

"You did well," she says. "Not the happiest-looking dancer, a little terrified, but the dancing was good enough."

"Thanks," I say sarcastically. "I always hoped I'd make a good exotic dancer someday."

To my surprise, she gives me a little smile.

CHAPTER NINE

"PHASE TWO IS GOING TO be a little more...difficult for you," Madame says as we stop back in the dressing room. She crosses to the dressing rack and starts rifling through outfits. "Though, I doubt you'll mind. At least you'll get to feed."

She stops on a hanger and pulls it out for further evaluation. Seeming to decide on it, the walks toward me.

"I don't understand," I say honestly as I accept the hanger from her.

"Don't worry about the details for now, just change." She doesn't wait for an argument from me. She turns to take care of the girls and boys that occupy the room.

Nerves eating me up all over again, I retreat to my corner and strip off the exposing clothing. I slip into the new outfit. This one is a black leather number. A halter style bra exposes all of my cleavage. A tiny skirt slips over a black thong, leaving most of my butt exposed.

I look at myself in the mirror. And I have to tell myself not to feel anything. That's the only way I'm going to survive these two days.

Madame yells over her shoulder in German at two men as she walks back over to me. The look she gives me is approving.

"That works quite nicely on you," she says, giving another false, tiny smile. "What you need to know about this next phase is that is the most expensive entertainment we offer at the Club, besides actual sex. Again, they are not allowed to touch you, but the paying clients will be sitting rather close so that they do not miss anything."

My heart hammers in my chest, and the palms of my hands prickle in anticipation.

"Don't worry," Madame says with that smile again. "The girls who get to do the biting rarely even notice the audience. Now," she says, stepping away. "Let me just go make sure your clients are ready and we'll begin."

She walks off, sweeping back yet another curtain. I wonder how many rooms and hallways break off of this changing room. She's gone only for a minute before returning. She returns with a beautiful redhead in tow. A human.

"I'd introduce the two of you, but it doesn't really matter, since you'll be leaving us soon," Madame says. "If you cooperate and survive. But this phase and task is quite simple. The two of you will go into the room together. You'll find a bed and an audience."

My throat leaps into my throat. My breathing speeds up. If they want me to have sex with this woman, I just don't think I can do it. I'll probably have my heart detonated.

A smile curls on Madame's lips. "No, you won't be having sex with her." As if she can read my mind. "You're only going to feed on her. I suggest you pace yourself. I really don't like having to replace the humans. So, take your time. These clients have paid dearly for this form of entertainment. They won't be happy if it's over in one minute. So, don't kill or turn her, and take your time."

The human woman offers me a little smile and reaches out for my hand. I feel sick as I offer it to her. This is wrong. So wrong. So dirty and twisted and carnal. I want to throw up.

But the woman walks down a hall with me, no hesitation at all. As if she's done this a thousand times before. As if she doesn't mind one bit what I'm about to do to her.

I remind myself what Madame said. This is the second most expensive service they offer here at the club. She might be getting bit every time, might have to take a few days off after each feeding, but she's probably making quite a bit of money doing it.

The whole thing is disgusting.

A black door waits at the end of the hall, and the woman rests her hand on it before she pushes it open.

Inside looks much like the rest of the club I have seen so far. Black walls, blue and purple lighting. But unlike the other spaces I've seen, a double-sized bed dominates the center of the room. And seated around it, are five men and one woman.

I try not to look at their faces as the redhead leads me to the bed, but I can't help it. Their eyes are hungry as they look at us. They barely seem human, the deeper I stare. They search my body, stare, smile over my crown.

They may be Royals. They may be Court members. But almost certainly, none of them are leaders. None of them hold real positions.

So they will get off, watching a Royal House leader being a whore.

The woman kneels on the bed and pulls me toward her. She smiles at me as I awkwardly crawl toward her. She rests a hand on my cheek, biting her lower lip.

The breath catches in my throat.

I just want to run.

I want to rip the hearts out of every single chest here and find an exit. I want to get as far away from the vampire world as humanly possible.

Because this...

This...

I was headed for this.

I did things.

Punished people in unfair ways.

Look at what I did to Samuel once.

What I did to poor, innocent Danielle.

I was only months away from falling completely off the dark cliff of losing my humanity.

But now I'm here. The King's prisoner. Now, I must bend to his will.

Just do this. Survive. Tell your story. And get out of here, I chant to myself as the woman pulls me even closer. As she guides my lips to her neck. As our audience leans in closer. As the hunger in their eyes goes wild. As my fangs extend and my toxins pool in my mouth.

As I let my teeth sink into her flesh.

Just survive this. And make it out of Roter Himmel alive.

IT DOESN'T TAKE LONG TO discover the Club never sleeps. Over the next twenty-four hours, I move from one room to the next. Dancing. Drinking from other women, men. Some of the faces in the crowd become familiar. And soon it seems I have a fan club. They just move from one form of my punishment to the next.

The crowd shifts throughout the club. People come and go. But it never seems to empty out. Even when surely daylight has broken outside once again.

There is an entrance to the outside. When I go back out on stage again, I see a door, way in the back, that opens to the dark, letting in fresh, pure air. I could run. I could make it. I'm sure of that.

But that remote detonator would go off, and then I'd collapse to the ground. Dead.

So, I dance. I drink.

The door opens just as I'm about to finish the seventh dance of my imprisonment, and my eyes flick toward it just as I twirl around the pole.

And I do a double look.

Because I know that face.

And it takes me a pole grind and my second attempt at a flip to place the time and place.

Five years ago, thousands of miles from here.

He walks in the Club, that same light smile on his lips that captivated me back then. That same amazing jawline. The same toned body.

It's only been five years, but my enhanced eyes can tell: he hasn't aged a day.

Fear pounds in my chest and my grip slips on the pole. I catch myself in time, and the music winds down. I make sure to keep my face down, turned away from the crowd. Anything to keep him from seeing my face.

Because if he does, if he recognizes me, it will be the end of so much.

I glance at him from the corner of my eye and see him make his way to the bar, his back turned to me.

The song ends, and I dart off stage as quickly as I can.

Tears prick at my eyes, coming hot and welling fast as I race down the hall. The breath rips in and out of my chest with determined speed. I break into the dressing room and immediately go to a dark corner.

In and out, I force my breath to go, otherwise I'm pretty sure I will stop breathing completely.

There are so many implications of this. So much that this means.

Natalia walks by, and I'm instantly on my feet, a hand on her arm, stopping her.

"All the clients at the Club are Born, right?" I ask, the words thick in my throat.

"Of course," she says, furrowing her brows at me. "Like I told you, they're all Royals. The employees of this club are the only non-Royal Born allowed in the city."

My stomach rolls. Heaves. I have to turn away. I race for the only bathroom and barely get to the toilet in time. A massive amount of blood heaves from my stomach and into the bowl.

"Pull yourself together," Madame says from behind me, in the open doorway. "You need to get ready for your last show. Then it's back to your trial."

I try to find the willpower to get up off the floor. I try to put it all aside and numb myself like I've become so good at doing. But instead the tears take me over. My shoulders quake, a sob rips its way from my chest.

Madame curses, turning her back on me. "You've got ten minutes. Deal with your shit and get back out here."

Sob after sob rips from my chest as she shuts the door

behind her. Fat tears roll down my face, and I wrap my arms around my middle, doubling over in emotional pain.

I closed that part of my life off. I haven't allowed myself to think about it in years. I made the only choice I could at the time and I moved on. I forgave myself and didn't look back.

But suddenly, the past has walked back up.

With shaking hands, I reach up and flush the toilet, sending half a dozen human's blood washing down into the sewers. I drag myself off of the ground. I stare at myself in the mirror.

I've ruined Natalia's beautiful work. Black streaks race down my face. My lipstick is smeared. My hair is a tussled mess from my hands running through it.

I'm a beautiful wreck.

A knock sounds on the door. "I can't wait any longer, Lady Conrath."

I take a deep breath in through my nose and let it slowly out through my lips. I roll my shoulders back.

I only have to pull it together for one more dance, and then they'll release me from this prison and send me to another where I can fall apart for good.

My shaking hand grabs thc doorknob, and I pull it open.

"Holy hell," Madame breathes at me. "You're a mess." She takes a deep breath, studying me with her hands on her hips. "I guess it doesn't matter for this last phase. Maybe you looking like this makes the effect even better."

She hands me another outfit, this one the most exposing of them all. I change without fuss. Without a fight.

Just make it through this last dance.

I grab my necklace from the pile of my clothes, and tuck it into the bra, unsure if I'll get the chance to return after. The thought of losing it now...

When I'm finished, I follow Madame through one last hall. The door at the end opens into a small room. Of course, at the center is a pole. A single chair sits in one corner. And dominating one wall is a massive mirror.

But not a single client waits inside. I look around, confused.

"You'll dance," Madame says. "For half an hour. Don't stop until the music does. Your clients wish to remain anonymous; they sit on the other side of that mirror. They can see you, but obviously, you cannot see them. When this dance is over, you'll be returned to await your trial."

I nod that I understand. She walks to the door and closes it behind her.

Thankfully, that numb feeling once more creeps up my legs, seeps into my chest, reaches for my fingers. I've been getting so good at it over the past eight months. Maybe it's because I've slowly been ridding myself of my humanity without meaning to. Maybe it's just who I was always meant to be.

I walk in front of the mirror, staring at myself. Imagining the sick perverts who sit behind it. Getting off on watching me. The types who comes to the Club often, watching men and women degrade themselves. Spending money on flesh they aren't allowed to touch.

The look in my eyes darkens as I stare at them, unable to see them.

Music suddenly sounds from the speakers, harsh and fast. One last glare at the window, and I turn to the pole.

I put all of my anger into this dance. All of the hatred I've felt for so long now. My insecurities and my fear. The manipulation I've suffered and the manipulation I've doled out. I let it all rip from my soul as I twist around that pole, bend over that chair, as I run my hands over my body.

Every single emotion runs out of me, channeled into numb sexuality. My brain shuts the people behind the mirror out, just focusing on me as I spill myself out into the curtained room.

The flashing lights dance over my exposed flesh. Blinking and racing around the room. I shut my eyes, just moving in rhythm to the music.

The song ends and another begins. I move. I don't think.

I bleed.

Three songs. Four. Seven.

On the eighth, the music slows, and I'm so engrossed in this dance of letting it all out that I hardly notice when the music has stopped.

I stand in the middle of the room, between the pole

and the mirror. Slowly, as I let my breath out, I raise my head back up. My hair parts around my face. And I open my eyes.

A light behind the mirror has been turned on, and suddenly, I can see through it.

King Cyrus stands right before me, a demented smile upon his face as he claps. Slowly. Deliberate.

And my heart drops into my knees when I see, seated on either side of him, is Ian and Raheem.

"Now that was a show," Cyrus breathes. The look in his eyes is gleeful. Wild. Vengeful. "I think we can all agree that was a wonderfully artistic display of the whore you are on the inside."

Ian lurches to his feet, his fists ready, but Raheem catches him before Ian can do any damage and throws him back into his seat. "Don't," Raheem warns Ian.

Cyrus chuckles, glancing back at them. "I thoroughly enjoyed the show, Alivia," he says. "But I don't think either of them appreciated it in the same way."

Something buzzes, and suddenly the mirror dividing us rises, and the rooms become one.

I back away a step.

I can't.

What I just did...

Everything I just laid out for the two men who matter to me most to see...

Something bites at the back of my eyes. Moisture pools in them instantly.

"Liv," Ian says as he rushes forward. He reaches out for me. But I take a quick step away. The look on his face is pained, but understanding. "Liv, I know that wasn't you. I know he made you do it."

I shake my head, one tear breaking free. I look over his shoulder at Raheem. And I see it there, in his eyes. He knows what's going through my head.

In so many ways, that *was* me.

I swallow hard, squeezing my eyes closed for a moment.

I don't want to be me anymore. I don't want to do any of this anymore.

"Come now," Cyrus says. I hear him take a step forward and open my eyes once again. "Don't try to act ashamed of your actions, Alivia. We all know how much you enjoy the attention. You certainly reacted to the way you and I danced, to my lips between your breasts. To Raheem pinning you against the bookshelf in your library. To Ian pressing himself into you on your kitchen counter."

The smile on his lips grows even more sick as the horror in me builds to an explosive level. "So why are you suddenly feeling so modest and prudish?"

"Stop!" I scream. The tears now freely flow down my face. "Please, just stop! I'm sorry, okay! I'm sorry I made you think I was Sevan. I'm sorry I needed you, Raheem. I'm sorry I fell in love with you when I shouldn't have, Ian! I'm just sorry!"

A sob takes me over, and I sink into a little ball in the

corner of the room. My knees curl up to my chest, and I wrap my arms around my head, attempting to block it all out as I sob, great big pulls of air and tears freefalling down my face.

"Enough!" Ian bellows as he crosses the space to stand by me. He crouches at my side, though he does not immediately touch me. "You may be our damn King, but do you have to be a monster? You've put her through enough!"

"My King," Raheem chimes in, "I understand how disappointed you are, but I do feel you've gotten your revenge. Can you not see the woman is humiliated?"

My entire body shakes. I didn't know that was still possible for my body. Which echoes the true measure of my pain. Cyrus does not say a word for a long minute. I hear the breath flow in and out of his chest heavily. Angry. Vengeful. Conflicted.

"Take her back to her room," he finally says. I hear his feet begin to retreat. "Her trial will resume at midnight."

His footsteps grow quieter and within moments, the King who has put me through so much emotional pain is gone.

"Liv," Ian breathes as he reaches out. "I-"

"Please don't touch me," I sob out. I flinch away from his warm hand, cowering all the closer into the corner.

"Liv," he whispers, but he does take two steps back.

"Would you like me to-" Raheem begins to say.

"Please, will you both just...go," I breathe out. I wind

my arms tighter around myself, squeezing my eyes tightly closed.

They're quiet. And I concentrate on calming my racing heart. On blocking the last two days out.

Raheem and Ian quietly talk to one another, but I don't process their words. And then, it's quiet.

For a while.

It's so peaceful. So empty.

But eventually, I hear footsteps come back into the room. A set of arms slide under my knees and around my back. My eyes flash open in panic for a moment as I'm picked up, my lips parting to demand solitude once more. But instead of Raheem or Ian, I find it's Markov who's come to me in what is surely my lowest hour.

"You're safe for now, my queen," he says in that low, calm voice of his. "You can rest your eyes now."

And I do. My eyes slide back closed as I rest my head against his shoulder, cradled into his chest like I am a child. As soon as he begins walking, the tears fall once more.

CHAPTER TEN

"I DON'T THINK SHE WANTS to see either of you right now," I hear Christian say in the bedroom. Markov glances at me once again before he walks out of the bathroom, where he's escorted me, closing the door behind him to give me privacy. "Just give her some space. She'll be okay. She always is."

Take these wretched clothes off. Toss them in the trash. Turn on the hot water. Step inside. Wash my hair. Scrub my body and face twice. Three times.

My skin is raw with the heat of the water and the intensity of my washing, but still I feel dirty.

I'm not sure I'll ever feel completely clean again.

Finally giving up, I shut the water off.

Awaiting me on the counter in the bathroom is a set of fresh clothes. A simple black dress, fresh underthings. I pull them on and open the door to the bedroom.

Markov and Christian stand talking to someone who quickly turns around. Trinity.

"I'm so sorry, Alivia," she says, taking a step away from me. "I had no idea what they were planning to do with you. If I had known what they did, I..."

"There was nothing you could have done," I say through a raw throat. I do however have a hard time meeting her eyes. "The King had a plan and no one could have stopped it."

"Still," she says. Her expression is crestfallen. "I'm sorry."

"Don't volunteer to be our leader's prison escort unless you plan on actually taking care of said leader," Christian says angrily.

"Don't," I say, shaking my head. "I can't handle any more contention. No more fighting. Not over me."

The fire in Christian's eyes instantly dies out, replaced with pity. Which I don't want, either.

"I'm really not that big of a deal," I say, attempting to lighten the mood. Because that's what I need at the moment. "Everyone should stop acting like I am one."

This does bring an immediate chuckle from Christian. And a hint of a smile pulls at Trinity's lips. Markov doesn't smile, but there is a hit of a twinkle in his eye.

"Okay," I say, composing myself. Crying time over. It just has to be. "How long until the trial resumes?"

"It should be any moment now," Markov says. "I do

believe they will send a messenger for us when the time has arrived."

"And you still won't tell me what evidence you've gathered in my defense?" I ask hopefully.

"Sorry, Livy," Christian says. "Not allowed to speak a word."

I nod my head, just as a knock sounds on the door.

"It's time," Christian says as he opens the door, revealing a guard.

I nod once, taking a deep breath. "Let's do this, then."

One by one, we file out the door, and down the hall, following the guard. I'm nervous, but only because for a moment, I'm terrified they will drag me back down into the belly of the castle to the Club again. Even the prison would be preferable. But this walk is familiar. I recognize the hallways and the rooms. And finally, we break into the room where I defended myself only two days ago.

It's set up differently. There's a raised platform at the head of the room, set with five grand chairs. Cyrus is seated in the center, Dorian and Malachi to his sides, Lillian and Elle seated, as well.

Before the platform sits a podium and on either side of it, a chair. And laying before all of that, is row after row of chairs.

And they're each filled with bodies.

A few hundred eyes shift to me as we step into the room. I feel their stares, their judgments, as I walk forward, flanked by a small fraction of my House members. I hold my chin high, my eyes staring straight forward.

The guard leads me to the chair to the right of the podium, in front of everyone, and my House has to take a seat.

A woman from the front row stands. Seated beside her, I see Ian and Raheem. They both look at me with worried expressions.

I look away quickly, because the humiliation rises back up in my throat.

The woman wears a classic suit dress, hugging her thin frame. Her honey blonde hair is done up in a twist at the back of her head. Her narrow face is hidden behind thick, horn-rimmed glasses. And the second she moves, I can smell how very human she is.

"Ladies and gentlemen," she says as she reaches the podium to my side. "My name is Alexa Vander Watson, and I have been asked to serve as facilitator at this trial. I am to be an unmotivated third party."

It's quite obvious, from the way she speaks. From her lack of fear or awe. She's a human, and all of us are vampires, and she has no idea.

"I've been told few details related to this case, so I remain un-swayed as to if the accused is innocent or not. While I will not make the final judgment, my job is to help the judges decide on the fate of this woman."

She clears her throat and looks out over the hundreds of vampires here. And suddenly, I remember what I was told as Trinity and I were brought into *Roter Himmel*. Less than five hundred vampires live in this little town. I would guess there are over two hundred of them here.

Almost half of the vampire population of *Roter Himmel* has come to witness my fate.

"It was on purpose that I did not attend the deposition of Lady Alivia Ryan Conrath," Alexa continues. "First, I will hear what the witnesses have to say. Review the evidence. And then, I will listen to the recording. A decision will be made exactly one week from today."

Seven days. After being here in *Roter Himmel* for thirty-seven of them, seven just doesn't seem enough to decide if I'm innocent or not.

But one way or another, all of this will be over in seven days.

"Those who wish to stand as witness in defense of Alivia, please rise," Alexa says, looking out over the crowd through her glasses.

The entire front row to my right stands. Christian, Markov, Trinity, Ian, and Raheem all rise to their feet. Five witnesses doesn't feel like near enough.

A moment later, Serge rises to his feet. A member of the King's court that spent over a month in my home. Tentatively, my heart swells. Perhaps I do stand a chance.

"Those who-"

"Sorry we're late," a voice suddenly interrupts Alexa from the back of the room. I look up to see Cameron looking around awkwardly, with slight awe on his face,

Samuel in tow. Samuel looks rather uncomfortable under everyone's very annoyed gazes. "We'll, uh, just take a seat. Sorry for interrupting."

Everyone continues to stare as the two of them make their way over to the other House members.

And I smile. Because now all of my original members, minus Nial and Anna, are here.

Even if Samuel is still looking at me like he isn't sure if I did this or not. Even if there's a little something different in the way Cameron smiles at me.

They're here. And that matters.

"As I was saying," Alexa continues, clearly annoyed. "Those who wish to stand in prosecution against Alivia, please rise."

Cyrus rises, his cold eyes fixed on me. Judith stands, Sebastian's poor mother. Morticia, Godrick. And to my horror, Charles Allaway, who I did not notice until now, rises with them.

Almost his entire House was slaughtered after leaving a party at my house.

He lost his twin sister that night.

I can't say I blame him for thinking I orchestrated their demise.

"Thank you," Alexa says, nodding her head to them. "The charges against Alivia Ryan Conrath are these: the creation of dozens of Bitten. Treason against the crown. And the attempted murder of King Cyrus."

For not knowing anything about our world, she says

all of this without hesitation or question. She is a professional to the end.

"First to the stand, we call Ian Ward," she says, looking up in Ian's direction.

He rises from his seat and makes his way to the stand. His long hair has been brushed back, his beard untangled and smoothed. He wears a clean pair of jeans and an old t-shirt. He doesn't look ready to stand as a witness; he wears no suit, he's dressed casually. But Ian in a suit is certainly a rare sight.

"Present your case to the masses and judges," Alexa says, fixing her cold eyes on Ian.

He runs his palms against his pants, looking nervously out over the crowd. "Um, I guess I'll start with Alivia's father. You all know of Henry Conrath, I assume. You knew his self-imposed isolation from the monarchy. I only met him a few times. And yeah, he didn't want anything to do with the system, but Henry was a good man.

"I think by now, most of you know my past: I used to hunt our kind, before I knew...knew what I was." He hesitates, his eyes on the ground. And I know the pain he's reliving. Discovering the truth about his mother's infidelity, her affair with some Born Ian will never know the name of.

"But for someone like me to respect someone like Henry, that says something about his character," Ian continues. He looks up at the crowd. "Henry had a dark past, it was known that he killed over thirty people the night his brother was betrayed and attacked by the people of Silent Bend. But he just wanted to stay to himself. I don't believe he ever wanted to bring down the monarchy. He just wanted to be left alone."

"And what about Alivia?" Alexa digs into the real issue at hand.

Ian's eyes slide over to me, and my heart does a little staggered backflip, as if it can't quite make it all the way over.

"So, what I'm saying is that even if Alivia had ever known her dad, it's not like he would have brainwashed her into wanting to take down the King or the system." His eyes dart away, back to those who listen. "When she came to town, she didn't know anything. Not even that she shouldn't go out after dark. Alivia was attacked by a Bitten just after she arrived. But I'd killed two other Bitten days before she even came to Mississippi."

"So, what is your assessment of Alivia's guilt, Mr. Ward?" Alexa asks. She stares at him through those glasses, the most intimidating woman I think I've ever seen.

"She's not guilty," he says without hesitance or backing down from her cold gaze.

"Thank you, Mr. Ward," Alexa says dismissively.

"Wait, that's all you want?" he asks, the pitch of his voice rising. "Alivia and I have nine months of history, and you only want two weeks of it?"

"Mr. Ward," Alexa says, leaning against the podium and angling her body toward him. "I have been informed of the relationship you and the accused have. While you may have been witness to a large amount of the time-frame, your opinions are biased."

"Are you kiddi—"

Ian is cut short when a guard grabs him and shoves him back toward his seat.

"Don't," I say quietly, meeting his eyes and shaking my head.

How many times have we done this? Him wanting to fight until he gets himself killed, and me talking him down, warning him not to get himself executed?

His glowing eyes stare back at me, the breath ripping in and out of his nose with speed. But he remains in his seat.

"You see why now, Mr. Ward," Alexa says, somewhat smugly. "Next to the stand, we call Charles Allaway."

My heart jumps into my throat. Charles rises from his seat, his cold eyes boring into mine as he walks past me to the podium.

"Please share with us your opinion," Alexa encourages.

"My sister and I came with half our House members to a party at the House of Conrath," he says, never once looking away from me. "It was an introduction, showing Lady Conrath off to our society. She seemed nice enough. Some events of the evening were unexpected," he says.

Unexpected indeed. Cyrus made us each trade five house members, and then fooled some of the others into thinking they could become members at Court, only to slaughter them for their betrayal of me. "But not from her."

His nostrils flare as his eyes burn into me. "Until we stepped foot outside. Until we made our way down the property, into town. Where we were attacked by her army. There were at least fifty of them, and only myself and three others escaped. The House of Allaway will take years to rebuild!"

He pounds his fist on the podium and the wood cracks.

"Alivia Conrath is a true Conrath, who hates the monarchy and everything our system stands for!" he yells, his franticness rising. "She planned this! She intentionally weakened my House!"

"Yet, who orchestrated that party?" Suddenly, Christian bellows, rising to his feet. His eyes flare red, his muscles tense and ready to rip some heads off. "The invitation came not from Alivia, but from Cyrus! I was with Alivia in the moments leading up to the party, and I have no reason to believe she was aware of anything that was about to happen!"

"Sir, you will sit down!" Alexa spits, harsh and loud. "You will be called to the stand when it is your time."

"I get you're pissed about what happened," Christian continues, ignoring her interruption. "I would be, too, if

I'd lost my brother that night and everyone else around me. But you need to take your emotions out of this because someone else's life is on the line right now."

"Enough," Cyrus bellows. A guard rushes up to Christian, who pushes him away and sits back in his seat without further encouragement. "If you interrupt this trial again, you will be sent home with a few missing limbs."

And to my shock, Christian doesn't look intimidated. Anger still burns in his eyes as he glares at Cyrus.

I'd almost forgotten what loyalty felt like.

And it comes from the member who took the longest to commit.

"Do you have anything more to add, Mr. Allaway?" Alexa asks, glancing back in his direction.

To my surprise, he doesn't seem so sure anymore. He looks at Christian, his eyes now heavily lidded, almost tired and defensive. He breathes slowly, quietly. As if he's contemplating everything that was just said.

"The attack was at her house," he says. "In her town. While I never saw her among the attackers, she certainly has the power to command such a bloody event. And she had the inside information to know we were coming and when to strike, with her *inside* connection of King Cyrus."

Without another word, Charles stands and quietly walks back to his seat.

But his entire last statement was quite unsure. So

timid and quiet. I'm not sure even he believed what he said.

"Thank you, Lord Allaway," Alexa says. "Next up, we call Trinity Dalton."

Trinity takes the stand with not a trace of emotion on her face.

"Do you believe Lady Conrath to be guilty of what she's been accused of?" Alexa asks.

Trinity doesn't look over at me. She stares straight ahead, deadpan expression on her face. "No," she says. And doesn't add another word to it.

"Do you have any evidence to back that claim up?" Alexa encourages, clearly aggravated.

Trinity lets out an annoyed sigh. She sits forward, resting her elbows on the podium. "In the beginning, Jasmine threatened Alivia. A lot," she says. "Myself, Christian, Samuel, Markov, Cameron," she says, pointing to the individuals she lists off. "Lillian. We were all part of this... broken house, led by this woman who wasn't a Royal. Jasmine really liked being in charge, so when she found out that Alivia came to town, and actually was Henry's daughter, and therefore the rightful heir to the House leadership, she really didn't like feeling threatened.

"So, she tried everything she could to twist Alivia into claiming the House, getting the Royal connections back, but not to actually lead," Trinity says. Her eyes look tired, disinterested. Once again, I feel her hatred for me resurfacing, and I still have no idea why it's there. "Things got a little extreme sometimes. Tense. In the end, Jasmine ended up killing Alivia's boyfriend."

"And how does all of this point to Alivia's innocence?" Alexa encourages.

"If Alivia had created this Bitten army and had them at her disposal, why wouldn't she have used it against the one person who was actually posing a threat to her?" Trinity says, finally looking over at me.

"So you've given evidence that she did not create this army," Alexa clarifies for the crowd. "What about the claim that she tried to have the King killed?"

"You should have seen her and Cyrus together the night they came to take Jasmine in, before they killed her," Trinity says. Her eyes glaze over as she stares at me. "They were a team. Bloodthirsty in the same way. You don't kill someone you get along with so well."

My stomach drops out into the center of the earth. Trinity has defended me in one way, but made me look so much worse in others.

But she's telling the truth. We were a pair of holy terrors that night. I was thrilled as I watched Jasmine fall. So satisfied when Cyrus stripped everything away from her.

I look back at Cyrus and find a gleeful smile on his face, him looking right back at me. "That was a fun night, wasn't it?" he says with a wink.

"Thank you, Miss Dalton," Alexa says with a dismissive wave.

Next, she calls a chain of the Court members who accompanied Cyrus to my House. They each get up, tell their stories, their opinions. There's a lot of repeating of the random attacks of the Bitten trying to infiltrate the House. The attack on the Allaways. And finally, the death of Sebastian in my own home, followed by the unearthing of the brands. And then, finally, the attack on Cyrus.

None of it is particularly new information. It's mostly retelling of what is already known. Those who accuse me have not known me long enough to say if they think I would do this or not.

And as they speak, I see the doubt in Samuel and Cameron's eyes lift. The evidence is weak. The motives missing.

I begin to feel hope.

Perhaps I will survive this trial after all.

Markov takes the stand. Speaking of the attack at the Broken House when I was there. Of how shocked I was, how confused about our world. Christian echoes his sayings. Talks of my leadership and what led to him joining the house.

There's nothing solid. Nothing to prove anything one way or another. The two brands, found in my house, stand as the only physical evidence, but there's an unsaid consensus that they could obviously have been planted. Because why would I be so stupid as to leave them out where anyone might find them and call me guilty?

"Next, we call on Raheem," Alexa says.

My nerves go crazy at his name. Because he's seen so much, even when I didn't know he was watching.

He walks to the stand and looks out over the audience. There's something different in the way he holds himself. His shoulders tense, a little downturn to his lips. Something is different, but I can't put my finger on it.

"At the end of last summer," he begins, his beautiful accent coming out strong as he speaks to the masses, "we received an anonymous letter to Court. This letter claimed that an heir to the Conrath name arrived at his estate just weeks after Henry Conrath's death. Of course, the King had a vested interest in discovering if this claim was true, so he sent me to spy on Alivia."

I look at him, and instantly, there is so much history in his eyes. There's the evidence of what he saw as he watched me. A woman, just trying to survive a new, supernatural circumstance. A woman falling for someone she thought would be her immortal enemy. A woman he learned to admire and long for.

"Everything that has been said today is true. I watched Alivia tirelessly after her arrival in Silent Bend. That was my job. To discover if the claim to Royal blood was true. If Alivia created a Bitten army, I would have seen it. I would have known. Because you all know my esteem." At this, his eyes darken. He searches the crowd, and a few of them do indeed nod their heads. Raheem is the most accomplished vampire spy there has ever been.

He's been in the King's service for over nine hundred years.

Of course his reputation would be widely known.

"You've obviously fallen in love with the woman," Godrick spits, disgust heavy in his voice. "We cannot trust your opinion any more than we can trust the others'!"

This causes a stir. Opinions fly into the air, slug harsh and heavy.

"It is true!" Raheem bellows over the crowd. "My feelings for Alivia Conrath have not remained hidden, as I tried to keep them. But the facts are the facts, and you will respect my long-standing reputation. All of these events were not orchestrated by this ignorant, infant of a Royal, but by whoever sent that letter to Court."

This stunning revelation silences every person in the room.

"I may have watched Alivia for months," Raheem says, glowering, his eyes flashing red. "But some other enemy has been watching her for far longer and has some very bloody plans. And Alivia is their patsy."

The room explodes. Shouts. Accusations. Defenses. Everyone has an opinion about this. My guilt. My innocence.

"Silence!" Cyrus bellows, rising to his feet. And instantly, the room falls quiet. "This information is surely fascinating. I think we all need time to process. Trial will resume once more in three days time."

He slams his fist down on the table, sounding a loud boom that brings this day's events to an abrupt halt.

The guards rush forward, and for a moment, I'm panicked. Last time I was taken from the trial, I was sent to a strip club. What can I expect this time?

But just as they grab me, a hand rests on my shoulder from behind. I look over my shoulder to see Dorian.

"Thank you, gentlemen," he says with a calm smile upon his face. "But I have discussed it with the King and he's agreed to release her into my custody until the trial resumes."

The guards give a little bow and back away.

I look back at him, wide eyed and surprised.

"Well, don't seem so shocked," he says, offering me a smile as he loops my arm through his. "You are a great-great something granddaughter of mine. I like to get to know my posterity when I get the opportunity."

I look over my shoulder, meeting the eyes of so many. They watch me, hesitant. Ready to spring to my aide. Ian. Raheem. Markov. Christian. And I don't know whether to reassure them or not. I didn't expect this.

"I assure you that you will be perfectly safe in my charge," Dorian says as he leads us out a side door. I glance over my shoulder once more, at all those who are on my side, before we slip out into a hall and they disappear.

CHAPTER ELEVEN

"I THOUGHT YOU MIGHT ENJOY getting to see a little bit of the town," Dorian says as we walk down a hall. "It seems a shame to come all this way, across the world, and not get to see such a unique and beautiful place."

"Um," I struggle for words. My mind is still reeling. Can I trust this man not to have a more sinister plan for me? It's hard to imagine he doesn't want to punish me, too. "Thanks. I'd love that."

"Have you yet had a chance to see the family tree?" he asks as we turn down a staircase and exit out into a hallway.

I shake my head. "I've heard about it, but I'd love to see it in person."

We turn right and step into a massive room. The stone floor stretches out long before us. Great tapestries hang from the walls and a dozen chandeliers hang from the ceiling. But the entire room is empty.

I walk into the room without turning my eyes just yet. I want to take the mural in as the grand spectacle it is. So I follow Dorian into the center of the colossal space before finally turning to take it all in.

And my eyes grow in wonder and amazement.

The wall has to be nearly fifty yards in length and the ceiling forty feet high. The span of it is colossal.

Indeed, the shape of a massive tree has been painted onto the wall. At the top sits Cyrus and Sevan's names. Branching down from them is a name that has been painted over. The brush strokes are violent, angry.

I once asked Cyrus what his son's name was, but he only became angry and told me his name had been erased from our history as if he never existed.

Dropping down from the blacked out name are seven other names. All but two of them are blacked out. Dorian and Malachi.

And from there, thousands and thousands of names branch out.

"It's beautiful," I breathe as I let go of Dorian's arm and step forward. While Malachi only has a few offspring, Dorian has so, so many. Raheem once told me that the seventh son valued power and worldly connections, while the third valued family. And the evidence is here before me.

My eyes travel down Dorian's line. So, so many

names. All my distant cousins. This strange feeling of connection builds in my chest.

All my life growing up, the only family I had was my mother.

But here. These people. They are my family, in some distant way. We share a common history. An ancestry. All of us.

As my eyes trace down one line, they finally come to rest on two names. Elijah and Henry Conrath.

Son of Colborn Conrath, who was one of three brothers.

Below Henry's name, the paint obviously much fresher than any of the other paint, is my name.

I reach up. Henry's name lies just above the height of my head, and I rest my fingers against his name.

"It is in your blood to want to connect with your family," Dorian says from behind me. "It is a terrible thing you were robbed of, never getting to know your father."

"I never knew I missed him until I saw a picture of him." The words tighten in my throat as I remember the first time I saw a picture of Henry back home. "But I do. Every day. I needed him and never knew it, for so long."

"My father was a power-hungry man," Dorian says as he stops at my side. "He did not love us children. We were tools to dominate the world. So I cannot say that I loved him. Perhaps that is why I desired so many children of my own. I wanted a family, to make things right. Family is direly important to our line."

I nod as I let my fingers fall from my father's name. "It is," I say as I look at him. "My mother and father are gone, but family isn't just blood. My House..." I hesitate as my heart hurts for them all. "They really are my family. I would do anything for them."

Dorian smiles at me. "And that is your defining characteristic as a third son leader."

I smile at him, appreciative of his understanding.

He gives me time to study the tree. I find many names I recognize. Raheem, a descendant of Malachi. X. The Allaways, who are also descended from Dorian. It's an odd feeling. Actually seeing the age, the physical connections in this visual form. To realize that I do know these descendants of a King.

"It really is incredible, the world and system Cyrus has created," I marvel as I take five steps back, away from the mural. "What he was able to create, thousands of years ago."

"Indeed," Dorian says. He offers me a smile and holds his arm out for me once again. "Come. Let us depart into the city while there is still darkness."

We walk through the castle. Down stairs, through hallways. The true size of the castle is well hidden inside the mountain. It feels as if it could be a city itself. I wonder what other secrets it holds, besides a prison, a strip club, and a multi-millennia old king.

I'm not sure I want to know.

Finally, we walk through a door and fresh air greets

my lungs for the first time in over a month. We step out into the courtyard, and I let my eyes slide closed as I take a deep breath in.

It's so crisp and fresh. So much easier to breathe. I don't feel like I'm suffocating.

"Lady Conrath?" Dorian says. I open my eyes to find him extending his hand toward a carriage.

A true blue, genuine carriage, pulled by two horses, with a driver and everything.

A smile crosses my lips for the first time in what feels like so long. I hold my dress up, careful not to trip on it as Dorian assists me in climbing aboard. I settle onto the padded seat and take in my surroundings.

The carriage is open air, no top closing it in. Two benches take up the space inside, and the driver sits in a seat supported by springs. With a gentle flick of the reins, he urges the horses forward. The wheels crunch over the cobblestones beneath us as we roll toward the gates.

Guards carefully watch us from the great stone wall that surrounds the castle. Weapons are generally aimed in our direction, but they do not look aggressive. That doesn't mean my eyes don't follow them.

But eventually, they fade behind us. The fields take over.

"These fields provide almost all of the grain the entire town needs year round," Dorian cuts through my thoughts. "Most of the humans who live here are farmers. Crops, animals. Some are shopkeepers. The town has lived in relative peace for nearly its entire existence."

"That's impressive," I state as we roll past the fields. Buildings begin to pop back up. "The humans must be treated well if they're happy to stay and work and be fed on."

"Generally, yes," Dorian says. "That isn't to say there haven't been incidents, but generally, Cyrus makes sure they are treated fairly. Above all else, he wants to keep our secret. That's difficult to do if you upset someone and they go off telling our town's secrets."

"How often do you visit *Roter Himmel*?" I ask. My eyes turn to the buildings that line the street we turn down on. "I heard you rule the House in Russia."

Dorian nods. "I do rule Russia. It's a big country with quite a Born population. It has been about seventy-five years since I've been to *Roter Himmel*, I would estimate."

He says it so off-handedly, as if it's only been a few months since he's been back. To his long, immortal timeframe, I suppose it is only a blink of an eye. But to me, that's when my human grandparents were born.

"Where are we going?" I ask.

"There really is only one place to take in the grand beauty that is *Roter Himmel*," Dorian says with a smile. He produces a box from beneath the seat and sets it between the two of us. "These are for a little later."

The wheels of the carriage roll over the dirt road as we head east. Houses become numerous. People come in and out. Whenever their eyes land on Dorian, they always fill with wonder, wide and surprised.

"All those who live here in *Roter Himmel* are Royals, correct?" I ask as I study them. They live in modest homes, have seemingly normal lives.

"That's right," Dorian confirms as he waves to someone.

"Do they not want the prestige of ruling a House?" I ask as I study the people. "Their lives here seem so... normal. All of the vampires I have met so far have seemed so...ambitious. I'm surprised this is enough for them."

Dorian looks away from the small crowd that has turned to watch us retreat away from them. He rests his elbow on the back of our seat and settles his chin into his palm. "We may be vampires, immortals. Stronger than any human being, more enhanced. But being accepted is still something we crave. To you, someone who has lived her entire life out there among the big, wide world, in normal society, it may be difficult to understand."

He crosses his legs, looking out over the city. "But most of the Born here have lived their entire lives in *Roter Himmel*. They were conceived here of the human female population. They died whenever they chose to. And they've lived an immortal life among others like themselves."

"They've never had to hide what they are," I fill it in.

Dorian nods. "Since you and I have always done it, we don't often realize how difficult a thing it is to ever conceal our true nature. To them here, it isn't worth it. They wouldn't know how to hide it, to not always act their true selves. So to them, the prestige of ruling a House isn't worth the lifestyle change."

I nod as I look back toward the crowd, which is now dissipating. "I understand that. Before I even knew what I was, I felt like an outsider in Silent Bend because the people treated me differently. And then, I began to build a few relationships, and not being able to be who I really was...it was painful."

Dorian nods in agreement. "We all need acceptance. No matter how old we are, no matter how Royal our blood."

"I completely get that," I say. And the words shake a weak fissure in my heart. I keep running into this issue, over and over again.

Our carriage breaks free from the houses, and once again, we are out into fields. I sense it more than see it as our elevation begins climbing gradually.

"Let me ask you a question," Dorian says. My eyes leave the beautiful landscape around me to look into his face. Dark hair, left slightly long. Brown eyes, similar in shape to Cyrus', his grandfather. Five o'clock shadow hugs his face, which is young, but not quite as young as me. I'd guess he's around thirty.

"Okay," I encourage him.

"You love Mr. Ward, who stood in your defense

today." It's a statement, not a question. "And it's blaringly obvious he loves you."

The statement hits me in the chest like a martial arts master. "I don't know if either of those statements are true anymore."

Dorian gives me a little knowing smile, a smirk even. "Tell yourself what you will," he says, which makes all my internal defenses bristle. How quickly I've gotten used to being a Royal and everyone being careful with what they say to me.

"I understand that he was once a hunter of our kind," he continues. "It's quite clear that he has a chip on his shoulder, as I believe the kids these days say."

I chuckle at that. Sometimes it's so obvious, the age of these ancestors of mine.

"So, I understand that things ended between the two of you, and it's obvious why feelings developed between you and Raheem. The look in his eyes when he stares at you..." I blush at this. "I've known the man for quite some time, and I've never seen anything but lust when it comes to him. But you...you've awoken something new in him."

The painful thorns in my heart dig all the deeper. "Do you have a point in all of this?"

"Please, my dear," Dorian says as he lays a hand over mine. "Do not be upset. I simply see a confused granddaughter of mine who is experiencing emotional pain. I only wish to help."

"And how is that?" My throat is thick as I force the words out.

"When you are released, returned to your House, because no one here truly believes you are guilty," he says it so off handedly, as if it should be obvious. My heart leaps into my throat, and I want to drag more information out of him, but he moves on almost instantly. "You will have to make a choice. Both of those men love you. Both would be willing to do anything for you. Do you know which one you would do the same for?"

There's that bite once more at the back of my eyes. My lower lip threatens to tremble just slightly. I refuse to let the tears well in my eyes, though. I just can't cry.

"Or has that decision already been made?" Dorian asks. "Maybe you already have done everything for one?"

On a night, months ago. When everything went so terribly wrong. When I walked into a House with my life on the line. When I offered it all in exchange for the distraction and the hope for time to escape.

"It was all for nothing, though," I whisper. "It didn't work in the end, anyway, and he still hated everything I became."

Dorian does not say anything for several long moments. He reaches forward, brushing a stray strand of hair out of my face. "It is hard to love something we have never loved before. To love something you once thought you hated. But learning goes hand in hand with time and effort. One passes without thought. The other is realized after all else. I do not believe it is time to give up hope, Alivia Ryan."

I shake my head, taking in a deep breath. "I don't think so," I say as my eyes dart away from his. "I've messed too many things up, toyed with too many plots. I think it is best I just step away from everything. If I survive my time in *Roter Himmel*, that is."

"Time is something we always have as immortals," Dorian says quietly. "If time is what you need, take it. Just remember, time is a key element in second chances. Time grants perspective."

I swallow, wanting both to push these emotions away and finally embrace them and let them consume me. "Can I ask you something?"

"Of course."

"You have many, many children," I say. "I know they are not all born of the same mother. Did you love the women you bore children with?"

My question must have been very unexpected. It takes Dorian quite some time to reply. He ponders, thoughtfully. It's understandable it takes him some time; he has a lot of it to consider.

"Before I could really even grasp what I was, what our race was, because then it wasn't even a race, I had fallen in love at a young age. We married. We had three daughters. And then, I died. I Resurrected with a thirst I cannot describe, yet you understand. My wife was there, eager to witness what my father promised when he murdered me. And I killed her."

I swallow hard. It's horrible. Yet apparently common. Jasmine did the same thing to her husband.

"Over my lifetime, I have had five human wives," Dorian says. "While none of them were my first love, I have loved each of them. And they, me. We had families together. We raised our children in a loving home. There are different kinds of love, Alivia. The kind we carry to the grave, no matter how long it takes us to get to that grave. It is the most intense, the brightest. And there is the kind of love that sustains us. It feeds us, lifts us up."

The carriage rises in elevation as we climb the foothills of one of the mountains.

"You are in such a unique position, my dear," Dorian says as we continue to rise. "You have experienced both. Both are *still* at your feet. You have a choice in this matter. I think you just need to look deep, and you'll find the answer."

I look away from him. Dorian puts these things into such simple words and statements. He's lived such a long life, loved so many and for so long. He offers words of wisdom.

"I can't accept that it will just be that simple." The words come out thick.

"That is because it won't be," he offers sympathetically.

That sense in the back of my brain begins to tingle.

The one that is ever aware of where the sun is. It rises, the sky lightening ever so slightly.

Dawn is not long off.

Dorian opens the box placed between us and offers me a set of sun goggles. I pull them on immediately, not eager to go through the torture I endured for a month again. And just as I finish pulling them on, the carriage crests onto a flat landing and the driver pulls the horses to a stop.

I've been so engrossed in our conversation, I haven't really taken in our surroundings.

"We have arrived," Dorian says as he stands and exits the carriage. He offers me a hand and helps me down.

The air is thick with dew and moisture. Trees surround us, glistening in the pre-dawn light. Flowers bud along the ground, weaved into the trees. The sound of rushing water draws my attention to the mountain-side, and I see a waterfall just to the north of our location. A river runs down the mountainside.

Birds chirp happily, ready to greet the day. A small noise draws my attention south, and I spot a herd of deer.

Here, on this leveled area, stands a gazebo. There is a singular swing installed, and Dorian and I take a seat on it.

And we gaze out over the beauty that rests before us.

The mountains rise all around the town. Covered in green, capped with white snow. They roll, smooth, and then jagged as they rise around us, protecting the secrets of this supernatural town.

The lake gleams in the dawn, huge and spanning. Little ripples wake out from tiny dots of movement. I spot three boats out on its surface.

And there are the fields. The animals. The homes and the businesses. And finally, the castle, nestled into the side of the mountain.

"It's breathtaking," I say as I observe every detail.

"*Roter Himmel* is a very different place from the one I grew up in," Dorian says. "We began to create something that wanted to be what it is today. And then the rebellion happened, and it was nearly destroyed. We are not a perfect people now, my child. You have seen our king. But we do some things right."

Such a complicated speech Dorian just gave.

So many good and bad things when it comes to the vampires.

Dawn creeps higher and higher into the sky.

And I hold my breath as it races down the mountain. As I wait for it to reach me and cause me endless pain and misery as I have come to experience over the last month.

But all I feel when it reaches us is warmth. Soft and calm. It caresses my skin, bathing over me. The goggles protect my sensitive eyes, giving me safe harbor from the intense rays.

And for a few minutes, I just sit there in silence, enjoying the beautiful dawn.

CHAPTER TWELVE

THE BUILDING WE DRIVE TO next is large. The closer we get, the more voices I hear. The more bodies I can sense inside. I realize just before we stop in front of it that it is a hostel of sorts. We climb from the carriage and walk through the front door.

Vampires mill about, sitting at tables in the common area. Ordering drinks from the bar at the back of the room. Chatting and laughing. Two human girls and one human boy wander through the crowds, acting normal and social, until some random vampire or another sinks their fangs into their flesh.

"They are all from different parts of the world," Dorian says quietly into my ear as we stand just inside the door, safely enfolded into the dark once more. "It's a rite of passage, in a way, for a Royal to visit *Roter Himmel* at some point in their life."

"I thought all the Royals away from Court ruled Houses," I say. "There are dozens of people here. They can't all be rulers."

"They aren't." Dorian takes a step down, entering the main room. He crosses to the bar and orders a drink. I follow quietly behind him. "You've seen the extent of the Royal line. There isn't need for so many Houses, and only the King's favorites live here at Court. Many Royals marry other Royals. Many are born into their parents' Houses. They are a part of a House, they have the Birthright to a House, but many do not actively rule."

I nod. "It's interesting to still learn so much about our world. And odd, that other parts of the world have an abundance of Royal leaders, when Silent Bend had such a shortage for over a hundred years."

Dorian smiles, finding humor in my statement apparently. "Ladies and gentlemen!" He suddenly bellows, causing me to flinch. His eyes have turned to the crowded room, and almost instantly, they look back at him. "I would like to introduce you to a new member of our society. She may only have been resurrected for a short while, but her blood runs deep. Say hello to Alivia Conrath, leader of one of the Houses in America!"

Several people do indeed shout a hello, their voices slurred sounding, overly happy. Others study me with curiosity. Suspicion. Surely, they know why I'm here at Court.

But not all. Others simply give me a little glance before going back to their business.

A woman wanders over, her red hair falling down her back in long waves. Her face is covered in splashes of freckles, her eyes vibrant green. She's breathtaking.

"You're a Conrath, ey?" she says. Her voice is heavily Irish accented.

I nod. Once more, I feel out of my element. I don't know what to expect from this room of mixed people. Will they hate me? Accept me? Not care one bit who the hell I am?

"I knew Lucas Conrath," she says. She must see the confusion in my eyes because she goes on to explain. "Henry and Elijah's uncle. Before the new world was discovered and they set off for the Americas, they lived in England. Lucas was one of the brothers that came across the waters to Ireland." She gives me a look, as if she's studying me. "You don't know much about your history, do you?"

I shrug. "I never met my father before he was killed," I say. "He left me very little, information wise. And no one will tell me anything. Apparently it was his wish."

"Ey, that's right," she says with a knowing smile. "He was the one who ostracized himself from everyone."

"That's one way to put it," I say. I'm so uncomfortable. I'm tired to being judged for the sins of my father. For being put in a box because he was different.

"Don't let everyone make you think he's the only one

in history who's walked away from the system," she says. "It's rare, but it certainly happens. Lord knows I get tired of it all and have to take a walkabout every century or so."

This does pique my interest. "Really?" I ask. It's as if a weight has lifted from my chest, and I suddenly breathe just a little easier.

"Course," she says. She takes a deep drink from her mug. "You stay around the same people for an immortal, long life and you get a little sick of them after a while. Who wouldn't need a break?"

"What is your name?" I ask. Confidence has begun to grow inside of me, the first I've felt of it since arriving in *Roter Himmel*.

"Siobhan," she says, extending her hand to me. "Of the House O'Rourke. It's a pleasure to meet another Conrath. It's been quite a long time. I'll admit, I had thought your line went extinct."

"We nearly did, I guess," I say. "Are there no other surviving Conraths that you know of?"

Siobhan shrugs her shoulders. "Not that I know of, but I don't exactly keep close tabs on everyone in the family. But if no one claimed your House after that long, I think it's safe to assume. Now, if you'll excuse me, that fellow over there needs some of my special attention."

She winks at me and looks over my shoulder to a dashing man with a devastating smile. Siobhan sets her mug on the bar top and walks over to him.

I watch her as she goes, so carefree and happy as she

and the man walk down a hall together. "Did you really mean it when you said that no one here really believes I'm guilty?" I ask without looking at Dorian.

"The King does love his games, especially when he gets the chance to mess with Royals without repercussion." He takes another long swallow from his own mug. "And more than anything, the attack at your House shook the Court members up. It's been a long time since they've felt unsafe. They're taking their fear out on you."

"So, they're just...toying with me?" The anger rises in my voice. A hot ball of acid grows larger and larger in my stomach. "Just...because they can? Because they're bored?"

"Well," Dorian says as he sets his mug down, the contents emptied. "I'm sure some of them do genuinely believe you did this. Sebastian's mother, for example. But only because they're too emotionally attached to the situation."

"This changes things," I say, my heart swelling. I can make plans now. I will be released. I'm going to go home.

"Don't get too excited," Dorian says. He waves the human male over. "You still have to finish out this trial. If you act overly confident, the King will likely drag it out just to torture you."

That's the last thing I want. They'll be finishing the trial in just a few days; I don't want to hang it up. I'm anxious to get back to my life.

And find who was trying to frame me.

"Lady Conrath hasn't fed in some time," Dorian says to the human man wandering between tables. He's blond, tall, fit. "Are you fit to feed?"

The boy says something affirmative sounding in German.

"Please," Dorian says, extending his hand toward the man. "I'm sure you are famished."

At the suggestion, my throat leaps to flames. My toes, fingers feel dried out. My fangs lengthen and the toxins drip from them. I may have fed, whether or not I wanted to, while in the Club, but I vomited it all out.

And now, I'm dying of thirst.

The boy does not hesitate. He raises his wrist and offers it without faltering.

My fangs sink into his flesh with no resistance. Instantly, my mouth is flooded with red warmth. A blissful groan escapes my throat as I pull. The liquid slides down the back of my throat, reaches out to every corner of my body.

In less than a minute, I am fully satisfied. I release the boy, who simply gives me a smile as the fog clears from his eyes, and he wanders away.

"You give an impressive show, Lady Conrath."

As I wipe any remaining blood from my mouth, I turn to see the woman who walks up to us. She's short and tiny, with flowing black hair and slanted eyes. But there's something in those eyes that looks deadly. After just a moment of evaluation, I know this is a woman not to be messed with.

"The way you've convinced your House members of your innocence," she says as she stops beside Dorian. "I will admit, you almost have me sure you've been framed."

"Then you must be someone who easily senses the truth." I lean against the bar, folding my arms across my chest. While it's been interesting to get to see different people in *Roter Himmel,* it's exhausting suffering all of their judgment.

"Usually," she smiles at me. Her accent sounds faintly Japanese. "But you are not a simple person, Lady Conrath. That much is obvious."

"There are very few simple people in our world, I've learned." I hold her eyes, blinking infrequently on purpose. This is something I've picked up: the appearance of innocence comes at my advantage. And any little ally I can make along the way at any point can come into play.

"It's true," she says as she accepts the glass the bartender sets in front of her. Dorian gives me a small glance before he steps away from the bar and settles at a table with three others. "Tell me, why are you being framed?" the woman continues.

"First, may I ask your name?" I say. A group of four get up from their table and make their way down the same hall Siobhan left. I indicate it, and the woman and I take the table.

"Not just yet," she answers me with a coy smile as she

sits. “I’d first like to decide if I want to give it to such a powerful prisoner.”

“That’s fair,” I concede with a nod. “I think the reason I’m being framed is because a civil war is coming. Someone has been building up an army. They’re attacking Born. They tried to take out an entire Royal House. They tried to kill the King. And I can only assume they are targeting me because they have something against my family.”

“The name of Conrath is an old one,” the woman says as she traces a finger along the rim of her glass. “Any House has many enemies if they’re ruling correctly. But your father’s seclusion is well known. You’ve caused some deep ripples in a short amount of time, Lady Conrath.”

I shake my head. “And that is my greatest challenge. Making people realize that this attack began before I even came into the picture.”

“A matter of days is an insignificant persuasion to those who have lived tens of thousands of them.” The woman leans back in her chair, crossing one leg over the other. Those dark eyes of hers study me in a distant way that is unsettling.

And there she’s illuminated one of my greatest problems. One I hadn’t really considered. To me, a few days makes all the difference, holds half of my defense. To me, who has only lived for twenty-three years, a few days matters.

But to these immortals, ones who have lived

centuries, millennia, a few days is nothing. A few blinks of the eye.

I need to focus my argument somewhere else.

"You say a civil war is coming," the woman continues after a few moments of my hesitation. "Do you have the numbers to win that war when it erupts?"

Her vivid picture drops a chill into my marrow.

So many bodies have fallen, so many lives lost, and we've not even seen the beginnings of the war Anna and I have predicted.

"No," I answer honestly.

"If you truly believe a war is coming and that someone has the numbers to put up a true fight, you need to try damn hard to make everyone see." She sits forward, resting her forearms on the table, looking coldly into my eyes. "This is how empires and dynasties fall. Because those who see the darkness rising from the shadows do not cry wolf loud enough."

A new fire ignites in my chest. I've been thinking so small. So central and so selfishly.

Because there is a war that is about to happen. I've felt it since I first learned about the Bitten. They've been enslaved in the dark, cursed with a Debt for as long as vampires have lived. I've seen evidence of the uprising all around me.

"I will," I say, nodding my head. "But I know they aren't going to listen to me while they think I am guilty."

"They won't," she confirms. "But that will be their

mistake. Often truth is realized when it is too late. I hope that is not the case for you."

She turns to the table next to us, says something in a language I do not understand to the people who sit there. An ancient man nods and hands her a stack of small pieces of paper.

She holds them out before her in her hand. I realize it's a deck of cards, but unlike any I've seen before. The paper isn't the thick, plastic-coated kind of playing cards I'm used to. It's closer to rice paper, thin and brittle. And there are only dots on the surfaces. No numbers, no kings or queens as far as I see.

"The King is not the only Royal who enjoys playing games," the woman says. She shuffles the cards, turning them and rotating as she does so. Her hands move so quickly they are only a blur. "While mine will not bring about bloodshed, perhaps it will stop some in the future."

She restacks the cards and sets them on the table between us. "I am a part of the House in Southern Japan," she says, looking up at me. "It is the third largest House in all the world. We have an army, one that I myself command."

It explains the coldness in her eyes, the deadly way she has been evaluating me tonight. Or rather, this day.

"We will each draw a card," she says, her eyes dropping to them. "Whoever draws the highest wins."

"If you win?" I ask. Anticipation and adrenaline spike in my blood. I sit a little straighter. I notice the attention of others has shifted to us. Their eyes flicker over in our direction. The room grows a little quieter.

"If I win, you buy me this drink and life goes along its merry way," she says with a little smile. "If you win, I swear to bring my army to your aid should this civil war come to fruition."

At the words civil war, the room turns silent. Every head turns in our direction.

"And why would you offer such a weighty prize?" I ask. My voice carries throughout the entire room.

"Because I love life," she says. Her eyes never once leave mine to search those that now openly watch us. She stays focused on me. "Because I am loyal above all to my kind. And I will not see either of those things threatened."

The weight in the room deepens, settling on each shoulder here with the intensity of the moon.

"Deal," I say, because I have nothing to lose.

The woman reaches out and takes the card from the top of the stack. She holds it up so only she can see. "A seven."

I settle my fingers on the stack and take the top card. I pull it to me so no one can see the dots.

Three.

Three dots.

"A nine," I lie.

The room is silent for exactly one second. And then, those around us erupt.

"She's lying!" some yells, though it's unclear if they mean me or the woman across from me.

"Look at her face!" another says. "It's a bluff."

"Show us the cards!"

If I lose, all I have to do is buy this woman's drink. I don't even have any money here. I'm sure the debt will be forgiven.

But if I win, it's a huge gain.

I put the thin paper card on my tongue, wad it up in my mouth, and swallow it.

"A nine," I say again, never looking away from the woman.

A thin smile curls on the woman's lips, and it gradually grows and grows. The look in her eyes is full of pure delight.

She lays her card on the table, face up.

Three dots.

Our onlookers go wild. Some in anger, some in delight. Some in disbelief.

A satisfied smile comes to my lips. I'm not the only liar and manipulator at this table.

"A nine," the woman says. "What a lucky draw."

"You shuffled the cards well," I say, lacing my fingers together and resting them on the table.

The woman nods once, bowing her head to me. "You are a most skilled player in this Royal game, Lady Conrath. I swear my armies aid to you, should this civil war arise. My name is Noriko."

“Thank you, Noriko,” I say, bowing my head to her in return. “Your willingness to give aid will never be forgotten.”

She stands, giving me one last, studious look, and heads down the hallway.

“Well played,” Dorian says as he moves from his table to mine. “That was quite the move, eating the card so no one could confirm or disprove if you truly had a nine.”

“It was a nine,” I confirm once more, offering him a smirk.

“Of course it was,” Dorian laughs with a smile. “That was quite an alliance you just won. The House of Himura is a powerful one. Noriko’s father is only two generations from Malachi. He has led his House for over twelve hundred years. Their army is vast.”

“She was right though, Dorian,” I say. “If a civil war is coming, the Royals need to be more concerned about it.”

“My dear,” Dorian says, laying his hand over mine. “Our history is a long one. This is not the only act of war the Bitten have waged against us. This unrest in your region will not be the last we encounter.”

“So, you are not worried?” I ask as my brows furrow.

“I’ve lived so long, my child, that I do not worry over much of anything. Time will soldier forward, our kind will continue on, no matter the small worries that arise.”

I study him for a moment. It’s impossible to grasp the ages he’s experienced from the lack of worry lines on his face. On the outside, he appears as any other thirty-year-old man. All his centuries of life lie locked up in his mind.

"I can't think that way," I say, shaking my head and pulling my hands away from him. "Not yet, anyway. There's a problem in my region. And all I can do is plan for how to defend against it. I have to take care of it."

"As is your responsibility." He nods his head, his eyes sliding closed.

A yawn suddenly erupts from my chest, and I drag a hand over my eyes, rubbing them. I slept only a day ago, but suddenly, I am exhausted.

"Come, my dear," Dorian says as he stands. He holds a hand out for mine, which I take. "You deserve a night of rest after the time you have had here at Court. Let us get you a bed to rest in."

Dorian talks to the bartender in German and a moment later is given a set of keys. He leads me down a hall, where a few doors split off and then lead to a staircase. We climb them, up three flights, before coming out onto a landing. Down to the very end of the hall, where he opens a door.

It reveals a simple bedroom with a queen-sized bed in the center. There isn't much to it, but it's clean—and free of anyone else.

"You can rest here tonight," Dorian says. "I'm staying in the next room over. I trust you won't run, as you'll never be able to stop doing so for the rest of your days if you do. You're this close to freedom. Don't mess it up now."

"I won't," I say, shaking my head. Running sounds exhausting. I can wait this out just a few more days.

"Goodnight then, Lady Conrath," Dorian says with a nod as he lets himself into the bedroom next to mine.

CHAPTER THIRTEEN

WHEN I WAKE, IT'S TWILIGHT. Dorian takes me around the rest of town. I talk with more people. Feel all the more judged. Make a few new possible allies. And once again, I am exhausted when we return to the hotel the next morning.

Once again, I sleep.

I dream.

Of schemes.

Of war.

Of blood.

Of love.

Of repentance.

Forgiveness.

Tears run down my face as I sleep. Even in sleep, I am exhausted.

I toss restlessly in the bed. In my dreams, I hear feet

shuffling over the floor. Hear demanding questions about my location. Hear a door break.

Only it's not in my dream at all.

My eyes fly open as rough hands grab me and a gag is shoved into my mouth so I cannot cry out. Wildly, I search for the faces of my captors. And find familiar guards. The same ones who dragged me down to the strip club.

I throw my legs out as they drag me out of the room, trying to hook my feet in the doorframe and stop them from hauling me away. It manages to halt us for about two seconds before one of the guards turns.

A huge, meaty fist is the last thing I see.

THE FAMILIAR SMELL IS WHAT first drags my consciousness back to me. Of forest and rain. Of time and thunderstorms.

And the smell brings a wave of fear crashing over me.

My eyes fly open, only to immediately be met by a set of red ones, just inches from my face.

"About time."

King Cyrus backs away from me, a cold and callus stare in his eyes as he folds his hands behind his back. He begins pacing before me. "I thought we were going to run out of daylight before we could begin the festivities."

There's a sudden rush of sound, a great *clack.* Instantly, beams of light pelt into the room, sending searing pains shooting into my brain. I hiss and turn away from the light.

But the screams that rip through the air around me instantly drag my eyes back.

Standing behind Cyrus, back across the room, are so many familiar faces.

My eyes burn and water as I take them all in, but I cannot look away.

Against a wall, their hands shackled above their heads, their ankles grounded to the stone floor, is every one of my allies.

In the center are Ian and Raheem. Beside them are Christian, Markov, Trinity, Samuel, Cameron. Even Lillian.

The noise I heard earlier was from doors in the ceiling, covers that blocked out the light, but now every one of my friends is bathed in intense sunlight. They each howl in pain.

"Stop!" I scream. I jump toward them, only to find I'm chained to a chair. I test my strength, only every time I press too hard against my restraints, my skin burns. "Please," I beg. "Don't hurt them! Do whatever you want to me, but don't-"

"Don't what, Alivia?" Cyrus says as he crouches down, his face only inches from mine. "Don't mess with their poor little heads? Don't toy with them?"

The room is plunged into darkness once more, the sunlight blocked out.

I almost hope I am her. Suddenly, my own voice echoes through the dark, reverberating against the stone walls. *The Queen. Because if I start remembering, if I can recall all these past lives Sevan and Cyrus had together, maybe it will make me forget the past few months.*

They are my own words, spoken a few months ago, just hours after Resurrecting.

"You hoped, Alivia," Cyrus says. Suddenly, light floods the room again, a single beam of it. It engulfs Ian, and he roars in pain.

"Stop!" I scream. Once again, I jerk against my bonds, but my skin sears in pain.

"You *hoped*, Alivia!" Cyrus yells. "I saw it in your eyes. More than once. You wanted to be her. You felt what began to build between the two of us."

Once again, the light is cut off and Ian falls silent. I wonder why none of them are saying anything. Why are they not responding to my calls? Why are they not begging Cyrus to end this?

Do you still wish things could be different? My voice echoes throughout the room once more. *Now that I have become what I was born to be?*

I squeeze my eyes closed.

How does Cyrus have all these things I've said? Did he bug my entire house? Recording every single thing I've said?

Of course, he did.

He's the demented King who's stayed in power his

entire, long life. He knows how to hang dread over people's heads, to manipulate them into doing whatever he wants.

"But even though I saw it in your eyes," Cyrus says as he resumes pacing back and forth, his eyes coldly staring on me. "You said this. Behind your King's back. Behind the back of someone you said you hoped was your husband!"

Light once more floods the room, and now it is Raheem who hisses in pain. His blood red eyes stare at the King with hatred threatening to melt us all.

We all have our roles to play in this game. But it's just a role. Not the truth.

I squeeze my eyes closed as something breaks in my chest.

My words are so damning.

Cyrus turns and stalks toward Raheem. Suddenly, he balls a fist and swings. Raheem's head goes flying to the side, blood spraying through the air.

"You were my most trusted spy!" Cyrus bellows as he keeps walking. "Centuries of secrets. And then this!"

My eyes, wide and terrified, go back to Raheem. I want him to defend himself. To say it wasn't his fault, that I led him on.

But he only silently stares back at me. Through the blinding sunlight he's bathed in.

Kiss me, my voice begs over the speaker system.

A sob bubbles up from my chest. A ragged and

powerful thing. Tears suddenly spring to my eyes and my shoulders shudder with the intensity of everything coursing through me.

My eyes slide from Raheem's to Ian's.

So much pain.

I wanted you to do it. I wanted you to be able to accept me. As I am. As I was born. Please.

Even now, all these months later, the desperation in my voice is remarkable. I was about to die a terrifying death, after all.

Ian is once again showered in sunlight. One single cry and hiss of pain escape his throat.

Give me some time. My words whisper out into the great room.

Suddenly, all the lights fly open and everyone is engulfed in sun.

The screams of pain are horrifying.

Lillian tries to wriggle out of her bonds, to back away out of the sun. To no avail. Cameron thrashes himself back, tucking his head into his arm in an attempt to block out the light. Markov bellows a hissing growl, deep and feral.

Christian glowers at Cyrus, silent and immovable.

He's torturing them. Because of me.

Darkness once more. All the coverings close up once again.

"Do you have any idea what you want, Alivia?" Cyrus' voice cuts through the dark as my eyes adjust to the darkness. "You wanted Ian. You tried to die for him. And then, you wanted to be Sevan. You wanted me to make you forget. And then you wanted Raheem. You let him risk his life."

My eyes adjust, and I see Cyrus walking through the dark toward me. Like a black panther, about to spring on his prey and rip my heart out.

"You lied to me," I breathe. And the words cause physical pain in my throat.

All the hard lines on Cyrus' face fall and something flickers in his eyes.

"None of this would have happened if you hadn't lied to me." My words are quiet. Tormented.

"About what?" Cyrus asks. He stops a few feet away, his hands folded behind his back.

Once more, my eyes turn to Ian, but I still address the King. "I asked you who did it. Who ended my life that night. You said it was you. And you told me he left."

The pain that pours out of me as I stare at Ian could fill oceans. It's there in his eyes, too. Every emotion we've ever evoked within one another. All the hurt and anger, but all the sacrifice and the beauty.

"Everything would have been different if you hadn't lied to me." I tear my eyes away from Ian to look at Cyrus once again.

"If you truly love him, would you have so easily walked into my arms?" Cyrus asks with a calculating look. "Would your lips so easily have found Raheem's? You claim love, but, darling, I've loved Sevan for thousands of years. You have no idea what it looks like."

"Yet you are the one who forced this immortal life upon your pregnant wife!" The scream rips from my lips, fight suddenly burning in my veins. "Was it love that brought about a curse that made you crave the blood of your former kind? Was it love that has brought her death, over and over?"

Cyrus disappears in a blur and a fist connects with my face, sending me flying backwards, tipping the chair and sending me skidding across the floor to crash into the wall behind me.

"How dare..." Cyrus pants in shaking hisses as he hovers over me, "you question my love for Sevan."

I lie on my back, bound to this chair, staring up at him. My body quakes in fear. His eyes glow, his entire body trembling in rage. I can feel the blood gushing down my face, flowing from my nose. I can feel the broken bones floating around in my cheek.

I never remember my boundaries when it comes to pushing King Cyrus.

"Do not test me," he whispers. "Do not mention my wife again or I *will* kill you."

The look in his eyes... Nothing in me doubts the promise he's just made me. I give a quick little shake of my head.

Cyrus grabs hold of the front of my shirt and hauls me

and the chair back upright, setting me in my original position.

Every one of my allies thrashes, their eyes wild, struggling to come to my aid.

"They're quite the loyal lot, aren't they?" Cyrus walks toward them, looking at each of them as he walks down the line. "I imagine if I hadn't drugged them, they'd all be trying to tear me to pieces. This really is impressive."

He turns back toward me and this time, it's Christian's voice that cuts through the room. *I was wrong, Alivia. You were indeed born to lead this House. You're a ruler, a true Royal. And if you will have me, I will follow you.*

Next, it is Lillian. *You look around you. You see those around you who love you. And that word, it's a monumental achievement. No one but Micah loved Jasmine. But what we do for you, us being here, even though* he *is here, that is love. That is loyalty and devotion. You trust in it. Because it's here, and it's real.*

Such a fitting quote Cyrus has chosen. Considering the circumstances.

"My House is my family," I say as tears roll down my face. "I know some of them think I betrayed or fooled them, but I love them. Each of them. I had...have nothing, except them. The money and the connections of being a Royal mean nothing to me. But having them, my family..." My voice trails off as tears consume me and I let my head fall forward.

"Then you should have protected them better," Cyrus

says. "You should have seen the problem lurking in your backyard, and you should have ended it. We protect the ones we love, Alivia."

Tears stream down my face. I take a sobbing breath and nod. "I'm so sorry. To all of you. I was protecting myself, when I should have been protecting all of you. I'm so sorry."

The sobs take me then, harsh, raking breaths ripping in and out of my chest as the tears free-fall down my face.

"Spare me the waterworks," Cyrus says, his tone bored. Suddenly, he yells something in German and a man walks in. The two of them stand with their backs turned to me. Cyrus accepts something from him, and the man leaves.

"You all swore allegiance to Alivia at some point," Cyrus says without turning toward me. He once more paces before my House members and Ian and Raheem. "You've been through much the last few weeks. You've doubted. Questioned. Well, today, before her trial is fully finished, you get the chance, once again, to declare your loyalty to the Conrath name."

Without turning in my direction, Cyrus extends a hand out toward me. "Who among you swears fealty to Alivia Conrath?"

He turns toward the line, walking to the end, face to face with Cameron. "Do you, my young fellow?"

Cameron's eyes are wide, wild. He can't say a word, but he nods without hesitation.

"Your first re-pledge," Cyrus bellows. And abruptly, he turns, and I see what he's been hiding in his hand. An iron rod, one end of it glowing red. Without a moment of hesitation, he sinks the hot end of it into Cameron's chest, directly over his heart.

Cameron cries out in pain, his body bowing away from the demented King.

When Cyrus removes the iron from Cameron's skin, I see that it is my family's crest. Set to the end of a branding iron. Just like the snake army brand that was planted in my father's home.

"Stop!" I scream, lunging forward once again in my chair and burning myself. "Please!"

"Do you swear allegiance to Alivia Conrath?" Cyrus says, ignoring me and moving down to Christian.

Christian stares back at Cyrus with hate and anger in his eyes. Deep, sharp breaths pull in and out of his nostrils. But he nods his head. And Cyrus presses the branding iron into his chest.

He moves on to Markov, who swears allegiance. And then he's on to Ian.

"This truly is a complicated situation, is it not, my good man?" Cyrus stands in front of Ian, staring into his eyes, his face all too close for comfort. "You loved this woman, but you also hate everything she is. Everything you are. But here you are, and situations certainly beget circumstantial chances of heart. Do you, Ian Ward, former hunter of vampires, Born and Bitten alike, swear fealty to Alivia Ryan Conrath?"

I swear my heart stops in my chest. The breath leaves my lungs and every limb on me goes cold.

Every person in the room holds a collective breath.

Ian's eyes rise from the stone floor to meet mine.

Three months of hidden love. An entire House after us. The lies of a King. The weight of a race.

It's all there in his eyes.

But after only a few moments of hesitation, Ian nods his head.

"Now this is love," Cyrus says, glancing over his shoulder at me with a wicked grin. And gleefully, he presses the iron into Ian's flesh. Ian's head falls back, a hiss of pain rushing out between his teeth.

I pull against my bonds, my lower lip trembling as the tears roll down my face.

Cyrus moves on from Ian to stand in front of Raheem.

"You made the choice to risk your life for this woman," Cyrus says, his voice detached and cold. "You made the decision to go behind my back, after centuries of working together. I would say your decision has been made."

He presses the iron to Raheem's chest, burning through layers of clothing. The horror in my eyes is complete as I look back at him, trying to convey through them how very sorry I am. For everything.

On Cyrus moves, making his way through Lillian,

Samuel, and Trinity. Each of them pledges loyalty. They may each hesitate for a moment, and I cannot blame them one bit if they pledge out of fear for their lives. But they each have the iron pressed into their chests.

"Such loyalty," Cyrus says when he turns away from the last of them—Trinity. "Alivia may not know what loyalty means when it comes to matters of the heart, but those who follow her certainly know the true meaning of the word."

He stalks back toward me. The red glow on the end of the brand has faded, though I still see the waves of heat that rise from it. "A solemn oath sworn under duress circumstances. Come dawn, when your trial resumes, none of them will remember any part of this special inquisition. But they will carry the scars, the mark of loyalty, for the rest of their lives. Binding all of you together, as family."

And Cyrus presses the iron into my chest. A scream of pain rips from my lungs, fierce and wild. I feel my flesh bubble beneath the iron, give way, and collapse under the pressure.

He pulls the iron away and tosses it into one corner of the room. With the snap of his fingers, every one of my House members collapses, as if they are dead. Guards flood into the room, one for each of them, and drag their bodies away.

"I do hope you are proven innocent tomorrow," Cyrus says as two guards come to free me from my bonds. "It would certainly be disappointing for your House if you're found guilty and put to death and all those scars are for nothing."

My legs seem to have forgotten how to work and a guard drags me toward the door. My eyes hold Cyrus' the entire time.

This is the true measure of our King. His brutality. The cold that lives in his heart.

And he's won.

He's broken me.

CHAPTER FOURTEEN

WATER DRIPS INTO ONE CORNER of the cell. *Plink. Plink.* Over and over, never ceasing. In perfect timing and rhythm. It in itself is a new torture.

I sit on the stone floor, my knees pulled up into my chest. Hard walls press against my back, and the chill in this pitch-black room is enough to sink into my bones.

I wait. In my head, I count seconds in an attempt to keep track of time, but my mind keeps going back to the hours that are slowly falling behind, when Cyrus hurt everyone I love, just to knock me down.

And it worked.

I feel cracked. Shattered.

For a while, I thought I knew what I was doing. I thought I was a good leader and could make the calls that needed to be made.

But all I did was lose myself. I became a terrible person.

All those recordings Cyrus played just brought to light how awful I really am. How I toyed with Cyrus to make my broken heart feel better. How I led Raheem on. How I let myself rebound when Ian cracked me. How quickly I doubted him.

And the things I did. Leading Cyrus straight to Jasmine because I couldn't deal with her myself any other way. How I so quickly resorted to killing Danielle in the King's twisted game.

I am an awful person.

I tuck my head into my arms, huddling as small as I can. I want to disappear into the center of the earth, where the core will melt me down and obliterate every cell that makes up the mess that I am. To be erased.

I'm tired of this existence.

MY BARE FEET PAD THROUGH the hallways. Turn left and my eyes focus on the platform, which bears my judges. I meet their eyes as they study me. Lillian, who rubs a hand over the new scar on her chest. Elle, who carries that blank expression she so commonly holds. Malachi looks bored, anxious to get this over with so he can return to Egypt. Dorian looks completely confident. And Cyrus, who has a glint in his eye, which tells me he's recalling everything he just put me through.

The guards lead me to my seat, which is positioned before the masses once more.

Everyone else is already in their seats. The hundreds of residents of *Roter Himmel*. My accusers. And there, on the front row once more, is my House.

The moment they see my face, they erupt.

"What the hell did you do to her?" Christian bellows. Markov is instantly at my side, his eyes gleaming, his fangs bared. Cameron crouches beside me, his fingers gingerly touching my broken face.

My lower lip trembles. They really don't remember what happened. Don't remember being tortured. Why they're branded. How the King hit me.

"Back in your seats!" A dozen guards spring from their posts, dragging my House members away from me as they each fight and rage.

"It's okay," I hoarsely whisper. "Please, don't fight."

Samuel's eyes dart from me to Cyrus, hate and anger burning the ozone. Christian shoves a guard off of him as he makes his way back to his seat. Slowly, as each of my House members look to me for reassurance, they return to their seats.

"This is a jury, a trial!" X bellows as she steps forward, her eyes blazing. "You all will quit acting like the American savages you are and remember you are in the presence of your King."

This only earns them more hateful stares, but the masses far outnumber my House. The air begins to quiet and the tension is held in check for the moment.

I look back at them, studying their poor faces.

They each hold an expression of confusion in one way or another when they look at me. Trinity's hand rises to touch her chest tenderly. Cameron pulls his shirt down to expose the brand and mouths, "What the hell?" to me. I mouth back, "Long story."

"Thank you for joining us once more." Alexa walks into the room from a side door, her heels clicking over the floor. "A verdict will be reached today, and if found guilty, Alivia Ryan Conrath will be executed at twilight. If found innocent, she will be released, allowed to return to her home with her House members."

I look around, and some seem nervous, but others look so confident. Dorian was so sure. And when I think about my jurors, I should have this. Lillian and Elle will certainly vote me innocent, and Dorian believes me so. That's the majority.

But I feel nothing. Just...despair and guilt.

"Only three witnesses will be called today," Alexa continues. "First to the stand we call Horatio Valdez."

My eyes grow wider as a man stands from the crowd.

Surely not the same one.

He walks forward, taking the seat that faces the crowd. Short, curly hair, dark, tanned skin.

"I understand you were planted as a surveyor during the month Lady Conrath was imprisoned."

"That's right," Horatio says. And his voice, it's the same one.

Horatio was never a prisoner that entire month we were locked away down there. He was a spy.

"And while you were with Lady Conrath, did she ever say anything to make you believe she plotted a coup against King Cyrus?"

Horatio shakes his head. "Lady Conrath said very little during her time in prison until the last few days. She fought with him, quite a lot," he points Ian out. "They certainly seem to have some issues between the two of them. That was the only time she discussed what happened in America."

"And with what this woman said, unknowing that you were sent to listen, do you believe she committed these crimes?" Alexa encourages.

Horatio looks over at me. "No." It's a simple statement, filled with confidence. "She told the story, exactly as it's been told to all of you. She was set up. Framed. While in prison, she attempted to get to know the prisoners, asked our stories. I believe Alivia Conrath to be..." Horatio pauses, searching for the right word. "Genuine."

"Thank you for your testimony, Mr. Valdez," she dismisses him. My brain is still reeling, trying to process this, that a fellow prisoner was really a spy. Is there anyone in this dark, red world that I can actually trust? Can a single person involved be taken at face value?

Alexa shuffles some papers behind the podium. "Our

next witness has just arrived in *Roter Himmel* and brings evidence with her to present. We next call to the stand Anna Burke."

The breath catches in my throat as I look around the room wildly for my General of security.

I hear a scuffle down the hall, and a moment later, Anna appears, dragging a woman behind her.

The woman thrashes, kicking her feet out, snapping her teeth in the air. When Anna drags her close enough, I see the woman's glowing yellow eyes.

Two guards step forward and help Anna shackle her to a chair. The woman snaps her teeth at them, twisting and writhing, kicking at whoever comes close enough.

"Is it my turn?" Anna asks with a heavy breath once she's secured the prisoner. She turns to me and her eyes widen in surprise. I can only imagine the sight I must be. I'm pretty sure Cyrus shattered half my face when he punched me yesterday. The bones have since healed, but I'm sure the bruises are something to behold. "Holy shit, what did you all do to her?"

Anna looks back at the judges, disgust and horror in her eyes. "Seriously, Lillian. You couldn't make sure they didn't beat her into a pulp?"

"It's not her fault," I say, my voice monotone. "She couldn't have stopped him."

And when I say him, every single set of eyes turns to Cyrus. Who only smiles. But no one says a word about it.

Anna shakes her head in disgust and turns back

around to face the audience. "I've been dealing with these Bitten for a while now," she begins. "And yeah, there are some suspicious things that make it look like Liv did this, but have any of you ever thought to ask one of them if she's the one in charge?"

She holds her hand out dramatically to the woman who's staring at her with death in her yellow eyes.

"Please state your name for the judges," Alexa instructs.

The woman only spits in Alexa's direction.

"Did Alivia create your army?" Anna asks, moving on, stalking in the woman's direction. "Did she do this to you?" She snatches the woman's arm, holding up her hand and exposing the snake brand on the back of it.

"I'm not telling you anything," the woman hisses between her teeth. She yanks her arm back.

"If Alivia was in charge of this army, all the soldiers would have to listen to her, would they not?" Anna says as she turns back around. "The Bitten have to obey their Debt, the compulsion to serve the one who turned them. So, if this army was Liv's, they'd have to listen to her. Liv, tell her to do something."

My heart jumps into my throat when every eye shifts to me. "Uh," I hesitate, my mind going blank for a moment. "Nod your head twice?"

The woman just looks at me with this dead look in her eyes and laughs. "When this war begins, you will fall. And you will weep at the feet of those you thought to enslave."

Her words fall like a heavy, wet blanket on the crowd.

Suddenly, Cyrus appears behind her, and with a quick snap and pull, he twists her head right off her shoulders. It lands on the stone floor with a wet thud. A moment later, her limp body collapses to the ground.

Cyrus' eyes glow brilliant red, his fangs extended, black veins running from his eyes, stretching down his cheeks like tiny snakes. "You dare bring a Bitten into my castle?" he glowers at Anna.

She doesn't take a step away, but it's obvious it takes everything in her not to do so. "I will prove Alivia's innocence," she says, with only a tiny waver in her voice. "She clearly has no power over them, so they obviously aren't hers."

Cyrus huffs heavy breaths as he stares at Anna. I'm afraid. I don't want him to kill her, but he will only be pushed so far.

"Adjourn for lunch," he suddenly bellows. Without another word, he turns and stalks out of the room.

It takes a moment for everyone to process the abrupt cut off. There's a moment of silence, of held breath, before a few whispers float through the room. Which builds into a murmur and then a roar. Bodies rise from their seats, following out of the room to head into another unknown location. Moments later, the scent of a feast wafts into our room.

"You okay?" Anna's voice comes up behind me.

I nod, though my eyes begin to glaze over. The numbness climbs up my legs, clawing its way into my chest, wrapping around my lungs. I see Ian and Raheem walk toward me, but I rise, and slowly back away. There's fear and panic in their eyes, but I don't have anything to give right now, and I don't have it in me to deal with them or to reassure. So, I continue backing away. Down the aisle without looking up at anyone. Toward the doors.

I wander. Empty. Cold. Finally, I find myself in a small room with no windows. There's nothing in this space. I sink to the floor, resting my chin on my knees.

Everything in life eventually spirals out of control.

And then, we find ourselves, here, at the bottom of everything.

I'm not sure how long I sit there. Letting everything bleed out of me. Dumping it all out. Forgetting who I am and that I am a being capable of anything, at all.

At some point a guard comes in to drag me back to the trial room. Literally, he hooks his hands under my arms, and hauls me over the stone floors, before roughly placing me back in my seat. I sit in my chair without a fight as we wait for everyone to file back in. I don't meet the eyes I feel on my face. I stare at the floor.

But I hear Christian and Markov whispering to each other. Their words don't process, but they sound worried. More and more people whisper, speculating.

One by one, everyone fills in. The judges take their places once more. Alexa takes the stand once again.

"As I understand it, those of the House of Conrath

have one last witness they wish to call. Is that witness here?"

Everyone looks around, searching the room for who the last witness might be.

"I...uh," Christian says as he stands. His eyes frantically search the room. "It seems our witness is running a little late."

"Or isn't coming." It's Samuel who mutters bitterly under his breath.

"The courtroom will not wait for a witness who is running late," Alexa says, with obvious annoyance in her voice.

"He'll make it," Christian says.

"He's obviously not coming," Samuel argues quietly. "He said he didn't think he should come, so obviously that's his answer."

"It's *Alivia,*" Christian hisses at him. "Of course, he'll show up."

"Gentlemen," Alexa says loudly. "This is not the place for brotherly arguments. If your witness does not take the stand in the next ten seconds we will move on, and the judges will make their call without hearing their testimony."

Markov stands, his eyes glowing deep and ember-like. The anger is obvious on his face. He looks around the room, desperate but unsure of what to do. He whispers something in Christian's ear, and he just gives a shrug.

"Five seconds, gentlemen," Alexa warns.

"I told you, he's not coming," Samuel whispers again as he argues with Christian and Markov.

Who else is left to speak in my defense?

Who are they all getting so angry about?

"I'm sorry, gentlemen, but whomever you're waiting for is obvious—"

"My apologies for being late." A calm and even voice instantly commands the room.

And my dead heart suddenly skips back to life.

My eyes rise from the floor to find Rath walking down the aisle toward me. His own, however, do not search out mine.

"I had a little problem with the guards at the entryway to the castle," he says as he takes the stand. He's dressed in an all black suit. His serious eyes don't seem to look directly at anyone. He shrugs his shoulders, straightening his jacket.

"Please state your name for the courtroom," Alexa says. She's obviously irritated at the bump in schedule and how she runs her trial.

"Rath," he says simply, as if he truly has never been anything more. "I have worked for the Conrath family for some time. I served Alivia's father, Henry Conrath, before he died."

"And you handle all of Alivia's financial affairs, is that correct?" Alexa asks.

"I left Alivia's employ a month and a half ago," he

states. And while he is normally so cool and collected, Rath looks tense. Nervous. Uncomfortable.

"And why did you leave?"

"We had opposing views on...things," he simply states.

A sting hits the back of my eyes. Moisture wells in them and I bite my lower lip. That really was the finest revealing moment of just how terrible I had become. When Rath told me he was leaving me because of my actions. Because of the death and violence I had brought back into my father's house.

"In the time you served Alivia Conrath, did she ever send any amounts of money that might look suspicious? As if she might be supporting a large number of people?" Alexa asks.

"In the six months I worked for Alivia, the only money she ever asked for was to build a low income housing development in our town," Rath says. He folds his hands in front of him. "If she had an army to support financially, I would have known."

Alexa nods. "And in the six months you worked for Alivia, how often were you aware of her location?"

"Alivia and I lived in the same house almost the entire time. It was only once she Resurrected that I left to give her time to adjust to her blood lust. But when I was not there, there was always someone from the House, or the Court, that was around."

"But you were not with Lady Conrath twenty-four-seven," Alexa confirms.

"No," Rath agrees.

I wish he would look at me. I wish I could get a moment alone to tell him how sorry I am. How much I want to take everything back. But I don't get that chance because he won't look in my direction.

"Do you have any irrefutable evidence that Alivia did not commit the crime she is accused of?" Alexa asks.

Rath blinks five times fast, licking his lips and swallowing hard. "It has been said that Alivia looks guilty because she—the Conrath name—has not yet suffered any serious attacks by this Bitten army." He fiddles with the cuff of his jacket. His body language screams sadness and unease. "But that is incorrect."

He's quiet for a long moment, and it's obvious he needs time to collect himself.

Suddenly, I am not so sure I want to hear whatever Rath is going to say.

"Please continue," Alexa encourages.

Rath clears his throat once more and looks up, though not at anyone in particular. "Henry Conrath was killed by someone from this Bitten army."

There's a deep, quick intake of breath from everyone in the audience.

"What?" the word slips out my lips.

"Someone broke into the Conrath house at dawn," Rath starts in again. There's a slight quiver to his voice. "I was just getting in for work. They staked Henry and then drug his body out into the sunlight to further the pain he was already suffering. I arrived just as they fled. I saw the brand. A snake, on the back of his hand."

I feel a million eyes turn to me, but all I can do is stare at Rath.

I knew my father was murdered, that someone broke into the house and staked him. But Rath never disclosed who, or what, killed him—Born, Bitten, hunter.

"Alivia has told you she knew nothing about our world before she inherited her father's house," Rath says. I see the whites of his eyes redden, well with moisture. "She isn't lying. Henry wanted it to remain that way. He never told her what she was or who he even was. These attacks started long before Alivia knew anything about this world. There's not a chance she's guilty of these crimes."

He places just a little too much emphasis on the word *these*.

He does hold me guilty of other crimes.

"Thank you, Mr. Rath," Alexa says. "You may take a seat. Ladies and gentlemen, we have heard the testimonies of numerous witnesses. Heard many stories and seen evidence. I turn sentencing over to our judges."

It's too quick. I'm not ready. I need time to process this new information. I need to think about what this really means.

But it's over now. We've reached the end of this trial.

And now, my fate will be decided.

"Lillian Summers," Alexa says and all the attention is turned to my first judge. "Based on the witnesses and evidence provided, how do you find the accused?"

I look at her, holding her gaze. She rubs a hand over her newly acquired brand again, the confusion evident. But there's also sadness. Regret. She was the first to doubt me when she was also the first to ally herself with me.

"Not guilty," she says, her voice sounding desperate.

I forgive her. Immediately and without question.

She's family. And that's what family does. We all make mistakes.

"Dorian?" Alexa asks.

"Not guilty," he says without hesitation.

"Malachi?"

Malachi's dark eyes study me. He hesitates in giving his answer. As if he's still evaluating me, determining if he wants to keep punishing me for something he may still think I did.

"Not guilty," he finally responds.

Chatter breaks out in the courtroom. A breath of relief is sighed from my House members, Cameron cheering loudly.

"Majority sets the judgment," Alexa says, cracking a small, forced smile. "Would the remaining two judges care to share their judgment, though?"

"Not guilty," Elle says. I manage a small smile for her, wishing I could hug her.

"King Cyrus?"

My body goes chill as I look back at my King and tormenter. The look in his eyes is so cold. So bitter.

I make myself a promise that when I get out of here, I will stay as far away from him as I can for the rest of my immortal life.

"I declare Alivia Ryan Conrath not guilty of the accused crimes," he says. And it's clear he, too, holds me guilty of other heinous acts.

"Then I officially declare Alivia Conrath free of any charges and free to go home to her House," Alexa says with a nod.

Noise takes over the courtroom and everyone has something to say to their neighbor.

I sit there. Stunned.

Numb.

I'm free.

CHAPTER FIFTEEN

My HOUSE MEMBERS RUSH FORWARD and there are so many arms around me, hands searching for touch and affirmation. I'm overwhelmed. Tears well in my eyes, and I'm having trouble breathing.

"Let's get the hell out of here," I hear Cameron say with a gleeful smile.

"The House is waiting for you," Markov says calmly.

A guard steps forward, knife in hand, and for a moment, I'm afraid. "Unless you want to go home with that explosive in your back," he says as he raises an eyebrow at me. I nod, and gently, he cuts into my skin, and I feel the pull as he removes the object. Next, he removes Ian's. Without another word, he turns and leaves.

Other words are being spoken, every one of my House members hardly able to contain their excitement. They're expecting my orders, waiting to be told what to do. To pack. To depart. To get a car and head to a plane.

Instead, I am only tossed about, still in my numbed and shocked state.

My vision glosses over. My ears are muffled.

I'm broken.

I can't be what they need right now.

"Give her some damn space."

Someone pushes the crowd away and then a strong, warm arm wraps around my waist. Which is good because my legs don't seem to be working.

Gently, they pick me up, cradling me into a strong chest. I let my eyes slide closed as feet walk over the floor. I feel like my head is spinning and I'm spiraling down, down through the center of the earth.

Maybe now I will get my wish. I will sink into the core, and then I will exist no more.

At some point, the noise of the castle fades away and I'm laid on a soft bed. I refuse to open my eyes, though. I just can't. I've dealt with too much for too long, and I've given all I had to give to survive. I'm empty.

Someone pulls a blanket up and over my body, though I'm sure I'll never be warm again.

But quiet is what I really crave right now, and I'm granted it. I focus on relaxing my muscles, one at a time. On slowing my breathing.

And at some point, I fall asleep.

• • •

WHEN I WAKE, I'M ALONE.

I sit up, confused for a moment. Over the last week and a half, I keep waking in different places, being shuffled from one room or prison cell to another. But I blink several times, clearing away the fog. And realize I've been in this room before. The one Markov and Christian came to me in.

Sitting on the end of the bed is a stack of folded clothes and a towel. Not allowing myself to sink into numbness again, I grab them and head into the bathroom.

I set my things on the counter and take three deep breaths before I find the courage to look up at myself in the mirror.

The entire left side of my face is covered in bruises. Complete blackness circles my eye, a finger of it racing over my nose, hiding under the other eye, too. Black and blue patches outline the ghost of Cyrus' fingers where he punched me, blossoming out from the impact site.

I raise my hand and gently touch the cheekbone. It's no longer broken, but I know he shattered bones. My nose looks ever so slightly crooked, it having been broken, too. My bottom lip is slightly swollen.

Vampires heal quickly, so the evidence on my face still there twenty-four hours later is a testament to how hard he hit me. I have little doubt his blow would have killed a human.

I wasn't prepared for the brutality of King Cyrus.

When Jasmine ruled the Broken House, they all were terrified to claim me because it would bring the King. I didn't understand their fear, then. I couldn't connect it with the honesty of his viciousness.

But here it is, full evidence, on my face.

Even worse, in my soul.

I turn from the mirror, strip, and step into the shower.

The clothes left for me are high class, fitting of a ruler. I feel an imposter in them. Black leather pants. A royal blue, flowing top. A high-collared, black leather jacket, which I leave on the bed for now.

I've just pulled my shirt on when there's a knock on the door. "Come in," I answer timidly.

I'm surprised when it is Raheem who walks inside and closes the door quietly behind him.

And as soon as my eyes meet his, I begin to cry.

"My *nofret*," he breathes as he crosses the room and gathers me into his chest. "This is a time for celebration, not tears. You are free."

I shake my head against his chest, wetting his tunic with my regretful tears. "There is nothing to celebrate. I'm a monster."

Raheem hushes me, holding me tighter. "You've witnessed a monster here, Alivia," he says quietly. "Do you really dare compare yourself to the likes of him?"

My breath comes in a shuddered, deep pull. He drives a good point, but I do not answer him.

"Cyrus has broken centuries-old Royals in much

shorter amounts of time," Raheem says as he gently sways me back and forth. "He's driven them to end their own lives, driven them into complete madness. You may not feel it in this moment, but you are *strong*, Alivia Conrath. You are here, on your feet."

"I feel like I've ruined everything," I confess.

Raheem shakes his head, his short beard brushing into my wet hair. "You've only gone through your first refiner's fire. You will come out stronger than before."

"I don't know," I counter. "I don't think I can go home and face it all again. I'm just walking back into a war."

"There have been no more plays since the night Cyrus was attacked," he says quietly. "I feel this is the lull before the storm. Take time if you need it."

The suggestion seems insane. How can I take time when the war is simply waiting to begin?

"I'm sorry, Raheem," I say, changing the topic. I have to deal with this guilt before it destroys me.

He hugs me tighter, pressing his face more firmly into the top of my head. "Do not be sorry. You only followed your heart. It's a fragile thing; we have to take care of it."

I pull away just enough that I can look into his eyes. And the tears flow down my face all the faster when I see the conflict in them.

"You love Ian," he finally says. His voice is quiet, strained, when he says it. But he does not falter. "Anyone who has seen the two of you together since your arrival in *Roter Himmel* can see it. It's deep and true, even if it's been complicated. You need to be with him, Alivia. You've been walking around with a great hole in your chest for months now. It's time to fill it back in."

I sob, my shoulders sagging forward, as he once again perfectly forms the words. I press my lips together, squeeze my eyes closed, and shake my head. I take a moment to compose myself. Finally, I open my eyes once more and look at him. "But you..." I sob. "You..." I can't form the words.

"I count myself lucky to have gotten the time I did with you," Raheem says, trying to look strong and sure when his eyes are telling me he's breaking inside. "We provided something to each other that we needed. We were a brief light in one another's world when the night was so very dark. I have no regrets, Alivia, and I do not wish for you to carry any, either."

I choke out a sob once more and collapse back into his chest, holding him tight. "What will you do now? Cyrus will not forgive you."

Raheem takes a moment, running his hand down the back of my hair. His breathing is calm, slow. "I am leaving the King's service. Court. The desert is calling my name. It's been too long since I've heeded it."

"You'll be careful, won't you?" I'm desperate for his promise.

"I will," he says.

I pull away once more and study his eyes. So deep and

rich. So full of secrets and time. “Thank you,” I breathe. “For everything.”

“Thank *you*, my *nofret*.”

And so very gently, filled with so much weight, I press my lips to Raheem’s, one last time.

Because there is no other way to say goodbye to someone who means so much to me.

Raheem breaks away, holding on to my hand as he steps back. There’s so much pain in his eyes. Love and need are never easy things. But there’s also hope.

After nine hundred years in the King’s service, he’s finally free.

In a terrible, horrible way, we freed each other.

“Goodbye, Alivia,” he says quietly.

“Goodbye, Raheem.”

The tears stream down my face as he turns, opens the door, and walks out of my life.

I sink onto the bed, my hands resting limply in my lap. Slowly, the tears stop rolling down my face. Slowly, my insides stop trembling. And one little breath at a time, a bit of my guilt and self-loathing releases from my body.

I stand, wiping a hand over my face, just as the door opens once more.

“Hey.” Samuel stands there in the doorway, looking very uncomfortable. “Uh, everyone is really anxious to get out of here. There’s a caravan waiting to take us to the plane.”

“Okay,” I nod my head. I wipe the remainder of the

tears from my face. I take one deep breath and grab my jacket from the bed. Sliding it on, I follow Samuel out into the hall.

And there stands almost all of my family. They watch me with careful eyes, expectant and ready.

"Let's go," I say, trying to give them a little smile.

I start down the hall, and one by one, they hurry to follow me.

Naturally, as if he was always meant to be there, Ian falls in at my side. We don't say a word, but I need him there. And I think he knows that.

A guard walks ahead of us, leading us through the castle. Down a hall, down so many flights of stairs. Across a huge ballroom. Down five more flights of stairs.

Finally, we walk through a massive doorway and out into the courtyard.

Many Royals wait for us there, standing in a line to the side of a row of cars. Cyrus and Dorian, Malachi, and X. Others.

My heart starts racing. I just want to be done with Cyrus. I hoped I would never see him again, and here he is, one last time.

The back of Ian's hand brushes mine, and instinctually, I grab for his fingers. I need something to ground me.

"I would be a rude host if I didn't make sure to say goodbye to such esteemed guests," Cyrus says with a cruel smile.

Every one of my House members tightens around me.

"It's okay," I lie, putting on the brave face. "Just get in the cars. We'll depart in a moment."

Their looks are wary, unsure. But one by one, they drop into vehicles.

Cyrus walks forward, leaving the others behind. "It's been an adventure getting to know you, Alivia Conrath," he says. I wish he would stop smiling. I want to make him stop smiling.

Ian must sense my rising emotions because he steps just a little closer. I hold up a hand, silently telling him to back away.

"And you, my King," I say. Miraculously, my voice does not quiver as it feels it wants to. "Your legend certainly does not do you justice."

Ian gathers a breath to speak, but I turn and meet his eyes with an icy warning. "Get in the car," I say through clenched teeth. We are down to the final moments of danger. I can't have him going and messing our departure up now.

The fight in his eyes is there, but he seems to sense how close we are now, too. Without a word, he slips into one of the cars.

"While it's been fun, these past two and a half months, marauding around with you and yours, I do hope it is some time before we have to have another face to face," Cyrus follows me as I walk toward the cars.

"You've certainly taught me a lot about myself," I say

as I stop, my hand atop the door to the vehicle. I'm so close. "About what it means to be a Conrath."

At my family name, Cyrus' eyes darken. "Hmm," he muses. "Rath's revelation certainly was interesting. And the timing was impeccable."

Something cold drops into my veins. "What do you mean?"

The smile quirks in the corner of his mouth. "Only that if a measly Bitten hadn't ended him, I would have killed the traitorous bastard myself."

"What-" I begin to question, my heart racing, but a hand reaches out from the car behind me and pulls me inside.

"He's just messing with you," Ian hisses.

My eyes wide and wild, I look back out at Cyrus. He bends down, looking inside. "I suppose you never know when it comes to me." He winks, smiling that wretched smile, and closes the door to the car.

"What..." I reel as the car rolls forward. "What did he mean by that?"

"I wouldn't think too deeply on it," Ian says, looking out the back window as we drive through the massive gates and across the bridge. "The torture of Alivia Ryan seems to be his new favorite game. He was just getting one last little jab in. Let it go."

"Where's Rath?" I ask, feeling frantic. "I need to see if he knows what Cyrus meant."

“He left just after your trial,” Markov says, and it’s the first I’ve realized he’s also in the vehicle.

“Let it go, Liv,” Ian begs. He takes one of my hands in his, rubbing firm circles into my skin. “You’re free. We’re going back home. Just let it go.”

“Let it go,” I repeat to myself.

But the words don’t connect.

CHAPTER SIXTEEN

I'M SILENT FOR THE REST of the drive around the lake, through the canyon, across the valley. Quietly, I board the plane with the others. I make my way to the back of it. Others try to sit around me, but I ignore them, looking silently out the window at the dark runway.

Ian sits in the aisle across from me. He never seems to look away from me, but he doesn't say a word.

The plane takes off. I watch out the small port window, my heart racing faster and faster as I see the runway whip by. And finally, the wheels lift off, and I am no longer on Austrian soil.

I close my eyes and lean my head back against the seat.

I'm free.

After almost seven weeks in *Roter Himmel*, seven weeks of uncertainty if I would live, I'm free.

But I am no longer whole.

Eyes closed.

Deep, slow breaths.

Just being.

We touch down at some point to refuel. Then we're back in the air and we all have to close our windows as the sun rises.

Just an hour before we touch down in Mississippi, Elle comes to sit down next to me.

"Hey," she says in that quiet way of hers.

"Hi," I respond. My voice feels rough, unused.

"Are you okay?" Her brows furrow with concern. She reaches over and takes my hand. Her skin is soft and warm. Warmer than I ever will be again.

I study my own skin for a long moment. The pores there. The little scar from where I cut myself in the bakery three years ago. The ragged state of my fingernails after so long without any luxuries. "No," I answer honestly.

Elle bites her lower lip, studying me. "I heard a lot of talk while I was in the castle," she says. "Most of those who are taken to the castle for trial don't survive. You're still here. And that isn't just luck. You're still here for a reason."

"Are you saying it's fate or something that I'm a shell of a person now?" My words are empty, hollow, and cold.

Elle takes a moment to respond. I can feel it as she collects her thoughts. So quiet and unknown. "When I harvest my garden, it looks terrible for a few weeks," she says. She rubs a circle into the back of my hand. "Ravaged. Mown down. It looks ugly. But it always grows back. It always reproduces. You've only been temporarily harvested and depleted. But you've got good roots, Alivia. You will grow back."

Once more, I'm tempted to cry. Such wise words from one so young. But I'm exhausted. And the tears will only drain me all the more.

"Where is Lula?" I ask, changing the topic. "Who is taking care of her?"

"The Sheriff helped me get her into a care facility," Elle says. There's immediate sadness and regret in her voice, which is quite the feat for her. "She's in Draper. She's technically a ward of the state until Ian comes back and decides what to do with her. He's her power of attorney. She's so far gone now, Alivia."

"I'm really sorry to hear that," I whisper. And I really am. The woman has always been wretched to me. Never a kind word or expression. But she took care of Ian and Elle after their parents were killed. She's strong. And that speaks for everything.

Elle nods, and this is the most emotional I have ever seen her. There's so much pain among those on this plane right now. It's crushing.

Elle pulls me into her and I rest my head on her chest as she wraps her arms around me. She holds me tight, and we cling to each other for the rest of the flight.

The wheels touch down and Elle releases me. Once

more, I get the feeling that I should feel stiff, achy, after everything I've been through, but this vampire body of mine is just fine.

Even if my mind isn't.

We taxi to a spot off to the side of the runway. Everyone pulls on a pair of sun goggles since it's only two in the afternoon, the brightest part of the day.

One by one, my House members file off of the plane. Ian waits until I stand and follows behind me.

Nial stands alone outside the plane, waiting. As soon as I see him, my heart swells.

As soon as he sees me, his doctor side goes into overdrive.

"What the hell did they do to you?" he breathes as he crosses the rest of the space between us. His fingers rise to my face, gently touching and feeling.

"I think I'm okay," I say. And it feels so nice, having someone genuinely concerned for my well-being. "The bones are healed. My nose might not ever look quite the same, but I'm okay."

He feels around, and there's a dull pain from his touch. "It does feel as if the bones have set correctly. That was some hit you suffered."

I nod. "How is everything at the House? Is Silent Bend still under evacuation?"

The rest of the House members load their baggage into the bus Nial has brought to shuttle everyone home.

"The snow melted about a week after Cyrus took you

away," Nial says. There's concern in his eyes, confusion, too. "Since the King and the Court members were gone, the Sheriff thought it would be safe to let everyone back into town. It's been a massive clean up effort to put the town back together. Things were a bit of a mess. We all did what we could to help."

"Thank you," I breathe, so appreciative. There was a reason I picked Nial to serve as interim House leader. "So the curse storm, it's gone?"

"It seems so, but there's something that just doesn't feel...right, in town," Nial says. "It's hard to explain. Like there's this gloom. This sense of dread that's hanging over everyone."

I don't quite know what to make of that. The curse storm dissipated almost as soon as I left town. Maybe it really was for me.

"Is everything else at the House okay?" I ask. "No more attacks?"

Nial shakes his head, watching as everyone finishes getting into the bus. "No more attacks. Things at the Institute are going well. We can finish going over everything when we get back to the Estate."

I bite my lower lip and glance over my shoulder at Ian, who waits silently. When I look back at Nial, he seems to understand what is coming.

"If things are okay for now, I'm not coming back. Not just yet," I say as I look away from Nial. "I've kind of...lost myself. I think I need at least a few days to go find Alivia Ryan again."

When I look back at him, he's studying me closely. As if he's reading everything I've been through right off my skin. He reaches forward and takes one of my hands in his. "You do what you need to do. We will take care of things, and your House will still be waiting for you when you get back."

"Thank you," I breathe. Tears well in my eyes once more. I pull him into a hug. "Will you tell the others for me? I don't think I can do it right now."

"Of course," he whispers as he runs a hand down the back of my hair. He reaches into his pocket and grabs something. When he places it in my hand, I see it's my wallet. And I have to wonder if he somehow expected this. "Go take care of yourself."

I step away, giving Nial a little smile. I turn back for the plane. Ian is at my side, and there was never any question that he was coming with me.

We walk back onto the plane, and I tell the pilot where to head.

Once we take off, Ian is on the phone, taking care of everything, preparing for our arrival. Once more, I close my eyes and revel in the quiet.

It's a four hour non-stop flight from Mississippi to Colorado. Twilight is heavy on the runway when Ian and I step off the plane and make our way to the small airport terminal where we pick up our rental car. It's a small, simple sedan, and for some reason, it's so comforting.

As we drive toward my old hometown, Ian reaches across the car and takes my hand in his.

Within twenty minutes, the surroundings become familiar. Memories start popping up to fit the locations. The doctor's office where I got my kindergarten shots. The movie theater we used to go to on Saturday nights. The diner where my mom worked.

"Turn left here," I tell him. Ian does, and we turn onto the road. Our hotel is just down the street. "Thank you for coming with me," I say quietly as he pulls into the parking lot.

"Of course," he says. His eyes are full of searching when he looks at me. But he doesn't press.

Without words, he knows I need some space right now.

We climb out of the car and head inside. Neither of us has any bags, considering we were both dragged away from our homes as prisoners. I only have the wallet Nial handed me and nothing else.

We check into our room and head up to the third floor. The hotel is standard, nothing particularly nice. This is a small town without many options, but it's clean.

As Ian closes the door behind us, I walk to the window and pull the curtains open, taking in the newborn night, staring out at the familiar town.

"So this is where you grew up?" Ian says as he walks

up beside me. He stands with his hands in his pockets, his stance easy and relaxed, but there is tenseness in his voice. He's not sure what we're doing here.

Neither am I. "Yeah," I say.

"This is the first time I've ever been this far north or west," Ian admits. "The clerk looked at me kind of funny. Don't think he liked my accent."

This does pull a little bit of a smile to my lips. "Southern accents do take some getting used to."

"So do you northern people," he teases me.

"Have you ever traveled much?" I ask absentmindedly. My eyes are running the familiar roads as the darkness takes over and the streetlights illuminate the town.

Ian shakes his head. "Only to Louisiana and Alabama. Never had enough money to travel anywhere else."

I shake my head. "Me, either. Here, and Utah to the National Parks; California once to go to Disneyland. Vegas with a friend a few years ago. But that's it."

"Well, now you can add Austria to your travel list." I look over and see a hopeful smile on his lips. He's trying to make me feel better.

But the reminder just brings up all the pain. All over again.

"Hey," he says softly. "I'm sorry. I shouldn't have brought it up. Come here."

He reaches out for me and pulls me into his chest. I'm panicked at first. We can't touch. We can't be close. Because I went and ruined everything. I made a mess.

But Ian voices none of those things. He only folds his arms tightly around me, guiding my head to his chest. And after a moment, I relax and wrap my own arms around his waist. I let my cheek sink into his chest. I take a deep breath.

This is so familiar, standing here, wrapped in Ian's protective embrace. Yet so foreign. We've been apart as long as we were together. It almost feels as if those two time frames cancel everything out. Yet there's too much history, too many emotions between the two of us for that to be true.

I'm not sure how long we stand there like that, just holding each other without saying a single word, but with each passing moment, the coiled black snake that has been living inside of me the past few months grows a little weaker.

CHAPTER
SEVENTEEN

"ARE YOU SURE THEY'RE EVEN still going to be open?" Ian asks doubtfully as we walk down the dark road. It's four in the morning; he's justified in questioning.

"This isn't Silent Bend," I laugh at him as I turn and walk down the sidewalk backwards. "The town's small, but not small enough that we wouldn't have a twenty-four hour LowMart."

He smiles back, entertained by my teasing. "If you say so, princess."

The words once came out of his mouth condescending and judgmental. Now they're just...light.

I smile once more before turning around again and rounding the last corner.

I'm not healed. But I'm trying. I need to laugh. To

shrug some of this weight off my shoulders. Even if it's just momentary. I'm going to try to fake it until I make it.

The store's parking lot is nearly empty. Half a dozen cars sit in the darkness, haloed in the pale buzzing glow of the lights that dot the concrete here and there. When we walk through the automatic sliding doors, it's a ghost town.

"You're a millionaire," Ian says doubtfully as we walk through and toward the clothing department. "You have half a dozen people who rely on you for their income. You're a damn immortal Royal, but you wanted to come to LowMart for supplies."

"It's time I went back to my roots, Mr. Ward," I say as I observe a stack of jeans that are only twenty dollars. I pick out my size and throw them into our cart. "I never had an item of clothing from a mall until I was fourteen and had the money to buy it myself. Mom didn't make enough at the diner for even mid-grade labels."

I grab a shirt that's on a plastic hanger, and debate for a minute if I like it enough to buy it. It'll do. I toss it into the cart, too. I grab two other pairs of pants and three more shirts.

"Trust me, I know all about bargain shopping," Ian says as he follows behind me with the cart. "I never bought anything that wasn't from a second hand store until I was a senior in high school."

"See," I say, looking over my shoulder at him as we keep walking. "We have at least one thing in common."

It's so simple and far too easy and normal for us. These conversations. Shopping. It feels fake and impossible. But how should it be? We were normal people once. I need that again.

"Yeah," Ian says with a little smile.

He follows me into the intimate wear section. And he blushes hard when I set to picking out two bras and a five pack of panties. I feel heat rise in my own cheeks when I toss them into the cart he's still in charge of.

"Your turn," I say, pulling the cart from him and steering us in the direction of the men's department.

"I don't know how I feel about you buying me stuff," Ian says, raising an eyebrow at me. He follows two steps behind me.

"You don't have much choice, considering you were dragged out of Silent Bend in the middle of the night. So, unless you want to wear those same clothes for the foreseeable future..."

He gives a smirk and relents to looking through the bargain-priced clothes.

He ends up with a pack of boxer briefs, two pairs of jeans, and a few simple shirts.

"I'm trying to imagine you here just a year ago," Ian says as we grab essential toiletries. Toothbrushes, paste, deodorant, shampoo. "Being broke, living by yourself, shopping just like any other twenty-something year old. I just can't really picture it."

"Well," I say as we walk down the shampoo aisle. "I

once knocked over this huge bottle of super cheap conditioner, right here," I say as I point to the exact place on the floor. "It busted open and spilled all over the aisle. I was too broke to pay for it and what I needed, so I just kind of snuck out of the aisle before anyone could see it was me who did it."

"You did such a thing?" Ian says in mock horror. I just smile back at him.

"Now you ready to see my ultimate human weakness?" I ask as I steer the cart in the direction of the food aisles.

"I'm pretty sure most everything about you was weak when you were a human," Ian says, his voice deadpan serious. "Except that time I tried to feed you to the alligators. Thought you were going to rip my balls off any second."

"I would have, had you suddenly not offered to take me home and make Rath explain everything."

I head for the snack aisle. My eyes scan the shelves until I find what I'm looking for. I grab the blue package of chocolate cookies with the milky white frosting in the center and hold them up in glee.

"For real?" Ian asks doubtfully. "You're like...this master baker, and you were addicted to this processed stuff that eternally gets stuck in your teeth?"

"I know!" I say painfully. "It's just when I have a package and a glass of milk, I just can't stop! I did hear once that these are more addictive than cocaine."

"Now, that's just ridiculous," Ian chuckles as he takes the package from my hands and puts it in the cart. He grabs one more off the shelf. "What?" he says defensively. "There's two of us and we're going to be here for at least a couple of days."

I just smile as I follow him to the refrigerated section, where we grab a carton of milk.

A few more snacks and food items later, we head for the checkout.

The girl that checks us out keeps giving me these wary looks. Mixed in with the appreciative ones she directs Ian's way. I give him a playful side-glance, and he just shakes his head with a little smile.

We pay for our stuff, and each of us with two bags, we walk back outside.

A light rain has started falling and the air instantly smells like the mountains.

"How far is this from the closest ski place?" Ian asks as we walk back across the parking lot.

"Ski place?" I make fun of him. "You act like you've never lived anywhere with snow."

"That's 'cause I haven't," Ian defends himself with a laugh. "I've never seen more than a dusting of snow, my entire life, until this year."

I chuckle and shake my head. "We're about thirty minutes away from the closest ski *resort*," I emphasize. "Take the highway over there, and you'll drive straight to it."

"You ever ski?" Ian asks.

"Our school took a field trip once when I was in eighth grade," I reminisce. "I was horrible at it."

Ian laughs at my expense, right when I hear someone walk up behind us. I turn just as the man pushes a gun into Ian's back.

"Just hand over your wallet and cell phone, nice and easy." The man speaks low, looking from side to side. We've just gotten out of the light of the parking lot and into the shadows of the road that leads off the side of the store.

Ian's eyes grow wide for a moment, and then a deep red ignites in them. And fear shoots up my spine. Not for Ian's sake.

"Sorry, man," Ian says with a little shrug of his shoulders. "But I don't have either of those things on me."

The man gives a frustrated grunt and pats down Ian's front and back pockets. When he confirms Ian is telling the truth, he shoves Ian aside, which is only accomplished because Ian lets him.

The man takes a step toward me, the gun pointed in my direction.

I let out a frustrated sigh. "And here I thought my week was getting better."

Ian moves in a blur and the man is suddenly hoisted up and over his head before smashing down to the sidewalk with a loud yelp. Ian yanks the gun from his hands, pointing it at the man's head as he places a foot on the mugger's chest.

"You picked the wrong two people to mess with tonight," Ian says. He's a terrifying sight. Slightly amused smile on his lips. Glowing red eyes. Toned body and tough-looking beard and long hair. I wouldn't want to mess with him.

"I'm sorry, sorry!" the man scrambles. "My mistake."

"Yeah, it was," Ian says with a chuckle. "Now, I'm gonna keep the gun, and you're going to go home and apologize to your mama for turning out to be such an ungrateful lowlife. 'Cause if you don't, I may come visit you in your sleep later on. You won't wake up feeling quite the same."

Ian takes his foot off the man's chest. He scrambles back and away from Ian, like an upside down crab. He falls in his haste to get away, flips over, and takes off running into the dark. He slams into a postage box, looks over his shoulder, and keeps on running.

"You enjoyed that way too much," I muse as we keep walking. Ian tucks the handgun into the back of his pants.

"Maybe a little bit," he says. "Gun wasn't even loaded."

I laugh, something full bellied and hearty, into the black night. Ian looks over at me, a full, bright smile on his face.

"This is nice," he says. "Just you. Me. Being normal.

Without all the extra pressure and supernatural shit. I feel like it's the first time I've seen both sides of the real you."

I look over at him, my mood sobering. His eyes glitter in the light, streetlights reflecting off them. He looks so easy. So comfortable. "I've never really seen you relaxed before," I observe. "I guess it's a night of firsts."

Ian offers a small smile and bumps my shoulder with his. And silently, we walk the rest of the way back to the hotel.

CHAPTER
EIGHTEEN

A SHOWER, NEW CLOTHES, A lot of cover up, and a good hair brushing later, Ian and I once again leave the hotel. We drive the six blocks east. There are only a few cars in the parking lot. No surprise when it's barely six o'clock and Robbie's Diner has just opened for breakfast.

"How long until the sun comes up?" Ian asks. His voice is nervous. And I can't blame him. He spent two months in a prison where he was tortured, every day, with the sunlight. As we walk to the front door, we're both very aware of the sun below the horizon.

"Probably just under an hour," I say. I'm nervous, too, but this is going to be our only chance to come. The days are too long now. "We'll be fine."

Ian nods, but I see him swallow hard.

We take a seat near the back of the diner and take the

two sticky menus from the rack at the end of the table. But instead of looking at the menu, I'm searching the diner for familiar faces.

But it's a young blonde girl who comes over and takes our order just a few minutes later. I've never seen her before.

"I remember you saying once that your mom had worked at a diner," Ian says. His eyes search the place. "I assume this was the place?"

I nod and motion him over to the wall next to the door that leads into the kitchen. Every inch of it is covered in pictures. The owner. The patrons. The waitresses and cooks.

I point to an old photo, faded and yellowed with time. "That's Mom."

Her hair is pulled back, her bangs big and poufy. Her uniform is stretched to the max.

"She was pregnant with you," Ian says. The fingers of his left hand rise up to touch Mom's round belly.

I nod. "She was supposed to start veterinary school," I say, a sad smile forming on my lips. "She made it through the first semester, even though she was so sick. But then she had to get a job. Robbie always said Mom reminded him of his daughter."

"Is this you?"

Ian's fingers have moved to a picture a little further down the wall, off to the right.

I can't help the smile that breaks out on my face. "Yeah," I say through a laugh.

In the picture I'm sitting at the bar, a milkshake in front of me. There's a hearty helping of ice cream dripping down my chin. My overalls are paired with my red Mary Jane's. My hair is braided into two sections, hanging long.

I've got this huge, cheesy grin on my face. Mom is on the other side of the counter, in her uniform, reaching and trying to clean me off. She has a huge smile on her face.

"You were a damn cute kid," Ian says with a chuckle. "You've got your mom's ears. Her chin. Definitely her smile."

"Not that you'd ever know if I had Henry's," I chuckle as I point at another picture of me and Mom. "I don't know that he ever smiled a day in his life."

"True," Ian says with a smile as he observes the picture of me, folding my arms over my chest, back to back with Robbie. We're both trying to look so tough. It's obvious he's humoring me. "How long did your mom work here?"

Once more, my eyes go back to the picture of her when she was pregnant with me. "My whole life," I say. "She was family here, and they took care of us. My grandparents died a long time ago, and Mom was on her own. But here, she had people who looked out for her. Who cared about her."

I feel Ian's eyes on me and it takes me a moment to read into the parallelism I've accidently drawn. But I don't return his gaze. I keep looking at Mom, letting a million memories wash over me.

"I knew that order of French toast and a slice of apple pie had to be Livy Ryan."

I turn at the squeal behind me and my heart breaks out into a happy sprint. Rhonda Jameson stands there with our order on a serving tray.

"Rhonda!" I squeal, rushing forward to wrap my arms around her bony shoulders. She hardly has time to set the food down before I tackle her with a hug.

"Dang, girl!" she says. "You must be working out these days."

"Sorry," I say, releasing her immediately. I take half a step back, resting my hands on her upper arms. It's been less than a year since I last saw her, but she's aged so much. Honey brown skin more wrinkled. The gray in her black hair more pronounced. The muscles on her body a little softer. "It's so good to see you."

"I can't believe you're back," she says with that wide smile. I slide into the booth, ushering her to sit next to me. "I mean, I always thought you'd be back, but then you never came home and I just thought you must have fallen off the face of the planet."

Her eyes flicker to Ian as he awkwardly sits back in his seat. "And I can only assume this fine gentleman is the reason why?" She gives me a look, waggling her eyebrows.

"Uh..." I say uncomfortably, because I'm not entirely sure how to answer the question.

"I'm Ian," he says, taking control of the situation. He reaches a hand forward, and Rhonda takes it with a suspiciously flirtatious smile on her face. "It's nice to meet you. I assume you were friends with Liv's mother?"

Rhonda looks so happy and giddy she could just shiver herself right out of her skin. She gives me a look, and says, "That'd be right. Marlane was my best friend. We raised two kids on our own, side by side. Working every hour we could get at this place."

"You never told me you had a near-sibling," Ian says as he looks at me.

"Oh, Livy and my Joshua were oil and water," Rhonda says with a laugh. "Two couldn't stand each other. They had to play nice when they were little, but as they got old enough, they just kept their distance. The diner was a lot more peaceful that way."

"Ah," Ian says insightfully. "So you had a mortal enemy early on."

I smile uncomfortably. "Guilty."

"So," Rhonda says, turning back to me. "You stayed down in Mississippi, then?"

I nod my head. "It's kind of turned into home, surprisingly."

"Did you learn much about your father?" she asks, her brows furrowing. "It's such a shame you never got to meet him before he passed away. Your mother never said anything about him."

That weight drops back into my heart. That hurt and desire is never going to go away. "No," I breathe. "He was kind of an enigma. I really haven't learned much about his...personality."

I know some details. Ones I can never share with this woman who was practically family.

"Oh, I'm sorry, baby," she says as she lays a sympathetic hand over mine. "I know that must be hard."

I nod. I'm feeling these emotions once again that I don't want to feel. "So, how's Robbie these days? Is he working this morning?"

"Um," she says uncomfortably. "Actually, Robbie passed away about four months ago. Heart attack."

My own heart sinks. The man was like the only grandfather I'd ever known. The overweight cook and owner who laughed at everything, talked to everyone, and ate everything in sight.

"I'm so sorry to hear that," I say. And I really, truly am. "Did Gordo take over?"

Rhonda shakes her head. "Gordo sold it. It's this new kid who owns the place now. He's nice, but it's just not the same. I'm the only one left."

All the staff, who had for the most part worked here forever, are gone. Moved on. I've only been gone for nine months, but everything has changed.

"Life moves on," I say sadly. "I'm so glad you're still here and that I got to see you."

"Me, too, baby," she says. She leans over and wraps her arms around me. "I've got to get back to my tables, but please stop by and say goodbye before you leave, you hear me?"

"Yes, ma'am," I say with a smile as she releases me and stands back up. She blows me a kiss before heading back to work.

I pick up my fork and stab a heap of the apple pie. I put it into my mouth and look up at Ian.

He's studying me. Deep. Thoughtful.

"What?"

He bites the inside of his lip, his eyes just searching me. He doesn't speak for a moment. Just keeps looking at me. "I think I get it a little bit now."

"Get what?" Anticipation rises up inside of me. Dread. Nothing has been fixed between Ian and I. All the problems are still there. And I don't think I'm ready to deal with them just yet.

He takes a sip of his coffee, stalling just a moment before answering me. "Family has never just been blood to you," he says. He plays with his food, not looking at me. "Your whole life it was always just you and your mom, but it was also the people around you. The ones who looked out for you."

I stab a slice of French toast, but don't take a bite out of it. My eyes wander once more to the pictures on the wall. There's Mindy and Tamara. Jaydon. Robbie. These faces that I grew up with. Some people came and went, but there were always bright stars in my life. And just because they weren't in my life any more, didn't mean they weren't still family to me.

"I grew up in a tiny town where I knew just about everyone. They all judged each other and knew everyone's business," Ian says. He bites off the end of a piece of bacon and takes a second to chew it. "They knew about my family's problems, how much my parents hated each other. Knew they were dead, knew my grandmother was a crusty old woman who was raising these two little kids. I love the people of Silent Bend, but I also felt removed from them. But that was all me. I did that, not them. I clung so hard to this concept that no one but Elle and Lula understood. That it was us against the world."

His eyes rise to meet mine. "But it wasn't like that for you. It was you and your mom and Rhonda and Robbie. Love was love, no matter if those people didn't share your blood, huh?"

Emotion hits me in every corner of my body. A sting zaps the back of my eyes and they well. "Yeah," I breathe. And it's the truth. "That's exactly how it was."

Ian's own eyes redden just a little bit. He reaches across the table and squeezes my hand. "I think I get it a little better now."

And the truth is there in his eyes. He's never understood how these flawed Born who had done terrible things for someone else came to be my family. How quickly they found a place in my heart.

But there I see it: he does understand now.

I've shown him my past. Shown him my roots.

And he finally understands.

CHAPTER NINETEEN

I CAN FEEL THE SUN sinking in the sky outside. It's still so odd. Being ever aware of where it is. Of how intensely it shines. I have an entirely new relationship with the sun. But I miss the old one where I could lay outside in it, soaking up the heat, letting it brown my skin. But those days are long gone.

I lie on my stomach on the double-sized bed and stare across the dark to the form on the other bed.

Ian lies on his back, one arm stretched up and lazing across the top of his head, which is turned in my direction. His other hand rests on his stomach. His shirt has worked its way up, exposing two inches of toned muscle.

My eyes search his face, studying. The three months of beard growth that hugs his jaw. The longer hair that falls around his face in a wild mane. The small lines that have already formed in the corners of his eyes from so many years of worry. Nose that's slightly too wide for his face. Lips that are pursed, as if he's having a bad dream.

There's so much that I miss about our past. The passion and the excitement of sneaking around. The stolen moments at night in my bed. The measures that were always held back.

But so much of what we were back then wasn't real. Ian and I, we are such complicated people, and only time and trial could reveal our depths. If we had continued without bumps as we had before, we never would have discovered the truth of what the other held.

It's difficult to say I'm grateful for everything that we have gone through.

But I think all this fire was necessary.

We may never be anything again, it's almost impossible to imagine that we can go back to anything smooth and gentle, but at least now we know.

And for the first time in so long, when I think about everything that Ian and I are, a little smile crosses my lips.

Careful to make my movements silent, I slip from the bed and head into the bathroom for a shower.

When I finish dressing, I find Ian waiting on the bed. "You get any sleep?" he asks groggily.

I consider lying for a moment, just to ease his mind. But the time for lies and deception are past. I shake my head. "Too much on my mind, I guess."

"That's understandable," he says as he stands. We

switch places, him heading into the bathroom. "What's on the agenda for today—tonight?"

"You'll see," I say soberly.

He doesn't question it. He only closes the door and starts the water.

Ten minutes later, we are driving toward the edge of town, towards the mountains. It's a quiet, easy silence.

Trees crop up out of the ground. The commercial buildings drop away. The houses become fewer and more spread out. The air grows crisper. We turn off the highway, before it starts up the canyon, and drive a little ways down the road.

Soon, there's a stone entryway with a great archway. An iron fence spreads out, encasing the huge plot of land.

Headstones dot the space before us.

Ian parks the car off to the side of the road and we both climb out. Twilight is fading away, darkness taking over. But our eyes do not falter, we have no troubles navigating our way.

My mother was buried toward the back of the cemetery. There are cemeteries closer to town, but this was the only one I could afford as a nineteen year old on a shoestring budget.

My heart pounds as we walk closer to where I laid her to rest.

"Are you sure you want to do this?" Ian asks as he takes my hand. He can hear my heart racing, smell the sweat that breaks out on my skin.

I nod, biting my lower lip. “I think I need the closure. Maybe then I can fully forgive what Jasmine did.”

Ian never lets go of my hand as we cross the cemetery, but I don’t feel his strong fingers holding mine. The numbness is starting to take over.

My eyes find the spot before we arrive. The ground is uneven. The grass has not yet begun to grow again. Spring has only just begun, there hasn’t been time.

We stop just at the edge of my mother’s former grave.

There’s a hole, as if the ground has sunken in. Which it has, because her coffin is no longer down in the ground. Raw dirt is mixed with the rain water, creating a puddle. It’s a sad sight.

“I wonder who got the new headstone,” I mutter. Because when Jasmine dug up my mom and had her delivered to my front steps, her headstone was also there. But sitting at the top of the grave is a new one. It’s simple. *In loving memory of Marlane Ryan*, it reads. Beside it is a bundle of wilted flowers.

“It sounds like there are a lot of people in this town who care about your mother,” Ian says.

“I’m a little surprised no one called me when the vandalism was found,” I say as I let go of Ian’s hand and walk to the headstone. I crouch down and trace my fingers over the headstone. It could have been Rhonda, probably was. Or anyone from the diner. Or our old apartment building. I can think of at least half a dozen people who would have helped pitch in.

"She's been gone for what, four years?" Ian asks. "It might have been a while before anyone found it."

I nod. It's true. "Wow," I whisper. "I can't believe it's been four years. I swear it was just last month that I got a call from the medical examiner's office to come identify her."

"One more thing we have in common, I guess." Ian's voice is low, quiet and slow. "Both our moms met violent, early ends. No kid should ever have to go through that."

"Our dads, too," I lament. "He may not have been your biological father, but he raised you, and that counts for everything when it comes to a dad. They were both taken too early. Well, I guess Henry had already lived several lifetimes, but still, taken before I got the chance to meet him."

"It's one extreme or the other in our world, I guess," he says. "Life is either way too short, or way too long."

I nod. It's all too true.

I settle back, sitting on the grass in front of the empty grave. Ian walks around to sit beside me. "Tell me about your life before you came to Mississippi," he says without looking at me. "What you were like as a kid. What you did in high school. You had this incredibly normal life when you were younger. I'd like to hear what that was like."

I look over at him, and he looks back at me. That desire burns deep in his eyes. While I never felt like my life was totally normal growing up, living in poverty, never knowing who my father was, I guess it's the story of many kids' lives.

And so, I tell him. Starting from as early as I can remember. My days in kindergarten. How I struggled with math. How summer breaks were so hard for my mom because she had to figure out what to do with me while she was at work. One summer, she surprised me with a trip to Disneyland; she'd saved up for over a year to pay for everything.

I recount my struggles to fit in in middle school. How awkward and quiet I was. How I finally found some good friends at the beginning of school, only to have both of them move away.

I tell it all to Ian. Exposing all the details. Every story I can think of, talking all through the night.

Except one story. Because I'm just not quite ready.

CHAPTER TWENTY

LIGHT BEGINS TO TICKLE THE horizon. We have at least an hour before dawn breaks over the trees. I lie with my head in Ian's lap. We don't say anything, I've run out of words and the past. So has he. He asked me to talk, and I did, but in the end, he told me all of his memories, too.

We're emptied out. Poured our souls out to lie barren on the floor.

In the middle of it all, I had to tell Ian how I killed Danielle.

I expected wrath. Anger. For him to storm off and leave me once more.

But he only offered a sad smile and squeezed my hand.

So now, with ninety-nine percent of everything laid out, Ian rises and extends a hand out to me. I take it, and once more, hand in hand, we walk back to the car.

I direct him back into town. Down one street, turning at another. And finally, we park along the road.

"We don't have much time," Ian says, his eyes turning to the horizon. Once again, we are pressed for darkness and minutes.

"I won't be long," I say.

Together, we walk into The Daily Fluff.

It smells heavenly as we walk inside. Of doughnuts and cinnamon rolls. Scones, coffee. It awakens so many memories and suddenly, my hands are aching for some flour on them.

"Morning!" a cheery girl I don't recognize says. "What can I get for you two?"

And I realize just how long it's been since I've fed. Eight days. Because suddenly all I can smell is the lovely blood under her skin.

"Uh," I stutter. I have to fight my instincts, to not let my fangs lengthen. Toxins pool in my mouth. Ian places a hand on my shoulder. He squeezes firmly. "I'll have a cinnamon roll and a latte. Does Jen still work here?"

The words come out in a rush, a mumbled, forced mess. Because my brain is tripping over itself, trying not to think about the warmth that could be cascading down my throat, but that's exactly what I'm focusing on.

"Oh, uh, yeah," the girl says. "She's in the back. Do you want me to go get her?"

The burn intensifies and I grip the counter to ground myself.

The girl gives me a wary look.

I've seen myself snap. I've gone out of control. I've drained people, gone too far.

"No, that's okay," I breathe out. "I just...wondered. Ian, would you like anything?"

"Just a coffee," he says, eying me, and I see it there, he's prepared to haul me out of here if he has to. "Black. To go."

"You got it," the girl says. "We'll have that in just a minute."

"Great, thanks," Ian says as he takes my credit card from me and pays the girl. "Wait in the car, I'll be out in a second." He breathes the words into my ear, quiet enough only I can hear.

I take off through the shop, stumbling into a chair in my haste to get out of here as fast as I can. I crash through the door with a little too much force, I hear the glass pop. My throat is on fire, and it's quickly spreading to my lungs, my belly. My arms are burning and my toes feel dehydrated as I yank the car door open and then lock myself inside.

I close my eyes and tuck my knees up into my chest. I securely fold my arms around them, locking my muscles tight, determined that I will not allow myself to move.

It feels like an eternity before Ian knocks on the

window for me to unlock the doors. He climbs inside and hands me my drink and food.

"That hit fast," he says as he sets his drink in the holder and puts the keys in the ignition.

"It gets bad sometimes," I say. My insides are quivering. My muscles are tensing, preparing for a chase, to hunt down some prey and drink. "Ian..." Desperation claws its way up my throat, and I'm sure I'm going to explode at any moment.

"Is there a medical center anywhere in town?" he says, action creeping into his voice. "Pretty much all those places keep a small supply of donor blood on hand."

I nod frantically. "Head north."

I direct him, feeling my thirst double, feeling the sun rise on the horizon. "Left here. It's there, see the sign out front?"

Ian nods and we pull into the parking lot. "Wait here," he says. There's fear and sympathy in his eyes, but I'm too thirsty to care. He climbs out of the car and takes off at a quick click to the back of the building.

I close my eyes once again, taking a sip of my scalding hot drink. It does nothing to quench my thirst. I take slow, infrequent breaths. The air on my throat only makes it burn hotter.

"They're humans, people, just like you used to be," I chant to myself. "They have families. Lives. You are not an animal."

I chant the words, over and over. My words grow harsher as my thirst takes over, driving my mind mad.

"You are not an animal," I growl. And suddenly, the driver's side door opens. My eyes fly open to see Ian climb inside.

And my Born side takes over as I rip the first blood bag from his hands. My fangs sink into the plastic and I take long, deep, frantic draws.

"It gets better about the three month mark," Ian says. He bites into his own bag and drinks. "It was pretty bad for the first two weeks, but it got controllable about three months in. You'll be okay in a few weeks."

But I hardly process the words. Greedily, I grab for another bag and down it.

Sensing the sun about to come up, Ian puts the car into drive, and we make our way back to the hotel.

I've just finished my third bag when we pull into the parking spot. Quickly, I check myself in the mirror. There's a drip of blood falling down my lip. My teeth are coated in red.

I take two seconds to clean myself up. The sun is just about to break over the horizon when we walk through the hotel doors.

Shame creeps up my throat as we cross the lobby to the elevators. Up until this point, at least Ian had never seen me succumb to my uncontrollable thirst. I've done so many other things to shame myself in front of him. I had hoped that I could at least avoid that one.

But now he's seen it all. All of my darkness.

The elevator closes behind us, and I let my hair hang in front of my face so that I don't have to look at him.

"Hey," Ian of course says immediately. "I am not going to judge you for being thirsty. We can't help it."

"You seem to be able to," I say, turning my face away from Ian.

"But don't go and think it's easy for me," Ian says, desperation rising in his voice. The elevator dings, and I immediately walk out and to our room. I slide the key card into our door and push it open. "Those first few weeks when I went back home, I made Elle watch me constantly. If I tried sneaking out to go feed, and I tried it eight times, I told her to shoot me with her toxins. Eight times I ended up lying in bed, in so much pain, just so I wouldn't go and kill someone."

"Why didn't I think about that?" I say to myself. I could have done that. Elle gave me some of her toxins, but the thought never once crossed my mind.

"Liv, the point is that I *would* have killed people if my sister hadn't stopped me," Ian says. He grabs my wrist as he sits on the edge of the bed, pulling me to stand in front of him. "The first few months of Resurrection are hell. Any one of the Born will say it. We just have to... survive, and hope the carnage we cause isn't too widespread."

I bite my lower lip, still not able to look at him. I sniff, fighting back all the emotions rushing through me. I feel too raw, too close to the surface. Being back home, being here with Ian...it's too intense.

"You say all these things like you've accepted them," I say quietly. "But I've seen the look in your eye. I've heard the things you say. Don't think I think you're just suddenly changing your opinions, Ian."

"Liv, look at me." His command is harsh, firm. It snaps my eyes to his immediately. "I've hated the vampires for my entire life because of what they did to my parents. They ended my childhood. But I've been blind to half my DNA for more than two decades. I had to deal with my mother's affair. I had to deal with the fact that my father wasn't my father. The fact that this world, these politics and curses, are a part of *me*."

I study his eyes, desperately searching for the truth. And I see it there in his gaze. In the depth of what he's saying.

"It took me a while, Liv, to accept what changed," he says. His voice is broken. Quiet. Sad. "And it's still going to take time, every day. But spending two months in prison, it gave me a lot of time to think."

Emotion makes his voice thick. His head bows for a moment. He squeezes my hands with his. And he sits like that for a long few minutes. I can feel the emotions, the weight of everything he's gone through. It chokes me, too.

Finally, he takes a hard sniff and looks back up at me. His eyes have reddened with emotion, his lips hard and tight. "And it made me realize what an ignorant ass I've been." Emotion bites at the back of my own eyes, but a tiny bubble of a laugh creeps up my throat, but thankfully, it stays trapped in my mouth.

"You were just dealing with what you had no choice but to deal with," he continues. "You were doing incredible things with your fate. And I just chose to be angry about it all, because I couldn't deal with my own shit. And the further I pushed you away, the worse I felt, every moment. I let it all eat me alive, fueling my anger and my resentment."

Tears break out onto my cheeks. Ian's voice grows thicker, strangled.

"And for the first few weeks, all I could think about was those few minutes when I came to you at your house, the night you died," he says. "How much it must have hurt you, when I asked you to leave with me and have a few good years." He drops his head down again, shaking it at himself in anger. "I can't imagine how that must have made you feel."

How it made me feel? Like my heart had just been ripped out, again. Then stomped on with cleats and kicked into a steel wall. It was worse than the death I would suffer just moments later.

"But when the King and Raheem rushed into the room just a few seconds later, I guess I had a moment of clarity," he says. Finally, he looks back up at me. His eyes are welled heavy, but there's simplicity in his gaze. "That you and I will never, ever be perfect. We will probably always have problems, and we'll probably always fight over stupid stuff. But I'd rather be with you, no matter how mortal or immortal you are, than not have you in my life."

My heart races and there are so many emotions rushing through my body, surely I will be swept away with the tidal wave, never to know which way is up or down again.

"Because," Ian whispers, "I love you, Liv."

I am a slave to my emotions and my heart.

My hands pull away from his and tangle into his hair as my lips take possession of his. Air is breathed back into my lungs for the first time in months as I press Ian back onto the bed and my body molds to every surface of his. His lips part and a hungry sigh slips between them. His tongue searches out mine, demanding and hopeful.

Ian's hands come to my back, running under my shirt, and surely the skin to skin contact will send me straight from this earth to a new, heavenly state of being. His fingers run over my depleted muscles from the last month and a half of imprisonment and deprivation. The bones of my spine send his hands up and down along the ridges.

Ian slides back on the bed, letting me ride on top of him as he does. Our mouths never separate as we move, and he rolls, so that we are side to side. His hand comes up to my cheek, carefully caressing it. His knee parts my own and rests on my upper, inner thigh.

Sparks ignite in my lower belly. A thousand tidal waves crash through my heart, a constant rush of rightness. My eyes roll back as his mouth moves from mine, down to my jaw line, and then to my throat.

"I've missed this, Ian," I moan. My back arches, aching to get closer, even though there is no space left between us. "Us."

He kisses his way down my throat, across my collar-bone. His hands come back to the hemline of my shirt and he lifts, moving his kisses to my stomach. I reach with my own hands and pull his shirt, sliding it up and finally, over his head.

He slides his way back up over my body, his skin brushing mine. He presses his lips to the hollow behind my ear, his tongue tracing over the skin as his hand lies flat on my bare stomach.

"You once told me that we'd been handed a miracle," he says as he pulls back to look me in the eye. "I was dead. You watched me die. And then, I wasn't. You and me, we are a miracle, Liv. Once we had an expiration date, and then forever. That's what I want, Liv. If you're willing to give me a second chance, I'll prove it to you that we're worth it."

Tears roll down my face; my emotions cannot be contained. I nod, unable to speak, as I guide his lips back to mine.

I thought this was over. I thought we'd burned too many connections, had too much anger, and made too many horrible mistakes. That there was no way we could ever find our way back to each other.

But here we are.

And all I can do is pray that it is for good. Because I can't survive another separation. Another broken heart.

He once again kisses his way down to my stomach, pulling my shirt off. The sun peaks over the trees in the distance, and the crack in the blackout curtains bathes us in dim light.

Ian slows as he kisses my skin, and I feel the mood instantly grow heavier.

"What..." he says in horror. "How did you get these scars? What did the King do to you?"

And my blood, which has been rushing through my body so hot, instantly grows cold.

"Liv?" he whispers. His eyes turn to mine, wide and horrified. "Did Cyrus-"

"No," I cut him off. Bile works its way up my throat and terror saturates my veins. I bite my lower lip and slide out from underneath him. I sit on the bed for a moment and take three deep, slow breaths.

"Liv, what is it?"

And his tone. It's so understanding and caring. So open for whatever I might say.

I'm terrified. I'm so scared of his judgment, again. But if we're going to make this work, if we're going to be open and honest with each other, I have to tell him my last, greatest secret.

I climb out of the bed, and turn on the lamp between the two beds. I stand there wearing no shirt, exposed for him to see so much of me. Ian's eyes immediately go to the two long, red scars on either side of my belly button.

"This is something I've never told anyone," I breathe. My hands shake. My insides quiver. And thinking about all the memories, my hands come to my stomach, as they once did. Two tears work their way from my eyes, out onto my cheek.

"Ian, I have a daughter out there somewhere."

The color drains from Ian's face and his eyes rise up to meet mine. He sits there in silence for several moments. Stunned. This wasn't the answer he was expecting. Not by a long shot.

"They're stretch marks," I say, looking down at the scars and running my hands over them. "She was a big baby; nine pounds, three ounces." A small smile comes to my lips as I recall her perfect face. The button nose, the pouty lips. Her huge cheeks.

I squeeze my eyes closed and let the tears keep rolling down my face. I feel Ian's hands on my hips and he pulls me toward him. He guides me into his lap, resting his chin on top of my head.

"I told you about it once, remember?" I breathe. Ian nods. "In my kitchen. I'd just broken up with my high school boyfriend. And I rebounded. This guy, he was at the movie theater where I'd been working. We talked. He asked me out. And one thing led to another. It meant nothing. It was a mistake." The tears roll faster down my face. "I don't think he even gave me his real name. And then, he was gone. And four weeks later, I realized I was pregnant."

Ian's arms tighten around me and he hugs me tighter to him.

"I couldn't believe what had happened," I say, shaking my head. "I'd seen how hard being a single mother was for my mom. I'd always told myself that I wouldn't relive the same mistakes she'd made. And there I was, even younger than she was when she'd gotten pregnant with me, and I didn't even know the guy's name."

I wipe a hand across my face, clearing the tears. "But my mom had done it, so I was sure I could, too. She said she'd help me. We could do it together. But then she was killed, and I was seven months pregnant and suddenly alone."

"Shit, Liv," Ian breathes. So much pity and pain in his voice.

I shake my head. So much self-hatred and regret coursing through my veins. "I knew I couldn't do it," I breathe. "I'd just lost my mother, the only family I'd ever had. I was grieving. I couldn't breathe. Could hardly function. I knew I couldn't take care of a baby. I couldn't be what a child would need me to be."

The pain I went through then, it was unbearable. The conflict and sadness and just everything nearly destroyed me.

"So I decided to give her up for adoption," I say, breathing out slow. "An agency helped me pick a nice family, here in Colorado, somewhere. They seemed perfect. Steady income, beautiful home. Strong family values."

"It was a great thing you did for your daughter, Liv." Ian says the words into my hair.

"I asked for a closed adoption," I say. "No contact. I didn't even meet the adoptive parents. Is that horrible?"

Ian shakes his head. "No. I'm sure it was painful enough. It would have been all the harder if you kept having to reopen the wound."

I nod my head, grateful for his affirmation.

"It makes sense now, your hesitance when we were together," Ian says. "I always figured it was because you knew I was a virgin, that you were just saving me. But you'd been through a lot of pain. I get it."

I'd told him once, when we were together intimately, on my kitchen counter, that I wanted to be careful. I was so scared of having sex again because the one and only time I'd ever had it, I'd gotten pregnant.

"Ian, there's something else," I say. I disentangle myself from his hold and move to sit on the bed across from him. My heart once more begins to race. "When I was in *Roter Himmel*, and Cyrus sent me to that strip club, I saw someone I recognized there."

I bite my lower lip. How it all came about, I'm still not sure, I can hardly believe it. "I saw my daughter's father in that club, Ian. I'd remember his face anywhere. He never saw me, I made sure of that. But I know it was him."

Once more, Ian's face pales. "In *Roter Himmel*..."

I nod. "I asked around. They don't allow just regular Born into the town. Anyone who comes to *Roter Himmel* is a Royal." I suck in a deep breath, wiping away the flow of tears. "Ian, my daughter is a Born Royal."

"But..." he struggles for words. "This just seems too impossible. What are the chances that you, a Born Royal, would get impregnated by another Royal before you even knew what you were?"

I shake my head. "I don't think it was chance," I say. And it makes me sick. "Because the odds are impossible. He knew, somehow, who I was. He had to. That's why I'm sure the name he gave me wasn't his real name. Some of these Royals are serial playboys, with their entire goal to create more Royal offspring." I shiver, feeling disgusting, knowing I'd fallen for the pervert's trap. "It makes me sick."

"Liv, that means if Cyrus ever finds her..."

"What he did to me...he'll do to her," I fill in as my eyes glaze over. "He'll want to see if she's Sevan."

The weighted silence in the room is thick and heavy. So many implications have been revealed.

"She'd be, what? Three years old?" Ian asks.

"She'll be four in two months," I say quietly. "On June second."

Ian stands and sits on the bed next to me, wrapping an arm around my shoulders. "Then we have time. He won't know about her unless someone says something.

Unless you claim her. And I know you would never expose her like that. So we have time. We'll protect her, Liv. I promise you."

The tears once more flow down my face. I let Ian pull me into his chest, and I just let him hold me. Because my strength has been depleted, and for once, I'm okay with my human weaknesses.

CHAPTER

TWENTY-ONE

I'VE FOUND HEAVEN ONCE MORE, and it is in Ian's arms.

I lie on my side, my knees curled up toward my chest. Ian lies behind me, cupped against my body. My head rests on one of his arms, his other draped over my side, his hand tucked under my rib cage.

He breathes slow, deep. For a vampire, he's been sleeping a lot. No surprise, considering everything we've been through in the past few weeks.

But I lie awake. My brain keeps running through everything, trying to sort through it all. Trying to plan. Trying to reconcile every choice I've made.

Ian is coming back to the House with me. We're going to be together.

I'd made Ian promise me once not to fall in love with me. But it was a promise broken before it was made.

I turn my head and kiss his arm. I haven't said the words back yet. *I love you.* But I do. And it's a relief to say them, even if it's just to myself.

After all this time, I can finally allow myself to fully love Ian Ward.

But I worry. The few days he spent in the House with my House members did not go smoothly. He and Markov nearly killed each other. I thought he was going to rip Samuel's head off at any moment. Can he get over his resentment of them? Can my two worlds of love and family ever come together peacefully?

There's a slithering eel in my stomach at thinking of my return to the House. When I was taken from it, I wasn't the person I wanted to be. I'd turned into a shell of myself, one who was so manipulative and dark that I was okay with living eternally in the gray zone of right and wrong.

I don't want to be that person.

But can I still be a ruler without using the tools I have in the past?

What is truly worth the effort?

Being a good person, the one my mother raised me to be, or fulfilling my birthright?

Birthright.

What will be my daughter's?

I don't know what to do with that, either. Will I someday reach out to her? Explain what she truly is? I'd wait years and years, obviously. Time is certainly the one thing that I have. But by doing so, I expose her to the investigations of Cyrus.

I understand now why my father did not reach out to me sooner. He was trying to protect me.

Just as a father is supposed to.

For the thousandth time, my heart aches. This is truly my biggest regret in life. That I never got the chance to know him. I want to hold Henry's hand, to look into his eyes. To tell him about my life. To have him give me advice.

"You okay?" Ian whispers in my ear, his lips brushing the skin on the back of my neck.

Instead of answering him, I roll back, my hand coming to the back of his head, and my lips search for his. They are met immediately—gentle, soft. His hand comes to my cheek, caressing it.

Nothing about Ian is gentle or tender, but that's exactly the way he holds me. As if I am treasured, prized. Coveted.

"Never again," he breathes softly into my mouth. "I don't want to wake up another night without you, Liv."

"Then don't," I whisper against his lips.

I don't know if it's a promise, an indication of something much more serious. But it's exactly what my soul needs to hear in this moment.

Ian props himself up on one elbow, looking down at me. He just stares at me for a long time, eyes tracing and memorizing every surface of my face. And I take my time appreciating him, this moment.

It's beautiful.

The lost, found. The broken, pieced back together to form something different. It resembles what it once was, but it's so much stronger.

Eventually, he looks up, his eyes going to the crack in the curtains. It's dark outside now, the time on the clock reading 11:23.

"I've got a few things to go grab at the store," he says. "I'll be back in a few, okay?"

"Alright," I say, brushing the back of my hand along his jawline, which is covered in his thick beard.

He presses a quick, light kiss to my lips, before climbing out of the bed. He pulls on the rest of his clothes, grabs the keys and my card, and winks at me before he walks out the door.

While he's gone, I shower and dress, and then set to cleaning our room up a bit. It's a mess. Clothes are strewn everywhere, shoes in the middle of the floor. Food containers.

When did we become such slobs?

I have a feeling we won't be staying much longer. I have one more stop, and then I will have no more excuses not to go home to Silent Bend.

Home.

It's felt that way for some time now. It's where my

family is. But knowing I will be returning with Ian by my side, it has taken on an entirely new meaning.

Ian returns forty-five minutes later with one bag and a bouquet of flowers.

"Would those be for me?" I ask with a sly smile. I walk toward him, accepting the beautiful buds he extends out to me.

"They're stupid, I know," Ian says, his face flushing slightly red. "But, I don't know. Nothing about us has ever been normal. Flowers are normal."

"They're not stupid," I correct him, stepping forward to take them from his hand. I lean forward and press a gentle kiss to his lips. "They're sweet."

Ian smiles under my lips, and a tiny chuckle bubbles from his chest. "And they may also be a bribe."

I take a step away from him, giving him a look. "A bribe? I don't like the sound of that."

Ian reaches into the bag and produces a set of clippers and scissors. "In exchange for taking a stab at this ridiculous mop on top of my head?"

I laugh, relief washing through me. "You want me to cut your hair?"

"Yes," he chuckles. "I don't know how you can stand to be around me like this. I look like a freaking lumberjack mountain man."

"Living around here, I've seen plenty of those types," I say as I follow him into the bathroom. "And I have to admit, you do kind of fit the stereotype at the moment."

"See," Ian says. "I can't go back to Mississippi as the cool, suave man toy of a vampire queen looking like this."

I just laugh, unloading the brand new clippers and length attachments.

I've never cut a man's hair before, but I'll give it my best. I set into his hair, first with the scissors because it's so long. And then move on to the clippers.

"Anything particular on the memory lane trip tonight?" Ian asks as he watches me work. I'd expect there to be nervousness or trepidation there, but there's just total trust.

"One more stop," I say, distractedly. I'm trying to blend this hairline and I don't want to mess it up.

Ian only nods and continues to watch me in the mirror.

It takes me quite a long time. I've never done this before and I'm so scared of messing it up. But in the end, it actually looks pretty good.

Ian runs his hands through his hair, eying it closely. "Nice work, Liv. I may have to keep having you cut it instead of Joe."

I shake my head, washing my hands in the sink. "Don't fire Joe. That was scary."

"You did great," he says as he presses a kiss to my cheek. "Now just give me a few minutes to finish up and we can get going."

I smile at him as I step out of the bathroom.

I sit on the edge of the bed and dial the phone number for my House. It rings five times before anyone answers.

"Hello?"

"Cameron, how are you?" I ask as a smile instantly crosses my lips.

"Liv!" he says gleefully. There are crunching sounds coming through over the phone and I'm sure he's eating something salty and crisp, as usual. "When you coming home? Things haven't been the same without you around."

"Soon," I say as I twirl the phone cord around my finger. "Probably in the next few days. Is everything okay at home?"

I hear sucking sounds, like he's licking the salt off of his fingers. "They're fine. Nial's a pretty good commander in chief. He's not you, though."

"Is that Alivia?" I hear Nial say in the background. Shuffling and irritated jabs, and a moment later his voice comes through clear. "Alivia, how are you?"

I smile once more. Just the sound of Nial's voice makes me feel calm and easy. "I'm okay," I say. "Better. How is everything going in Silent Bend?"

"Things have been pretty smooth, actually," he says. "It kind of feels like things are returning to normal."

"I'm glad to hear it," I say. "But I'm sorry to say, I don't think it will last for long."

"Nor do I," he responds. I hear others talking in the background. Anna, Samuel. Danny. "I'm not pressuring you, Alivia, you take as long as you need, but the House is anxious to know when you will be returning."

I sigh. It feels a bit like I am a mother and all of my children are starting to get rowdy without me there to keep them tame. "Soon," I repeat. "In the next few days, I think."

"That's wonderful." I think I detect a hint of relief in his voice. And I can't blame him. Leading a House is a huge undertaking, especially for one who's only known about our system for a few months.

"Thank you," I say. "For everything. I don't think any of us could have made it through this ordeal without you."

"It was my pleasure," he says, his voice always so genuine. "You took me in when I had no one. I can only repay the favor."

I nod, even though he can't see it. "Nial, I need you to do me one more favor."

"Anything." He doesn't hesitate.

I take half a second to speak. Because I'm not entirely sure how this will be received. "I'm not coming back alone. Ian will be with me. Can you tell the House that? Get them mentally prepared for him to join our family? I'm a little worried about how some will handle it."

Nial hesitates, and I hear a rustling on the phone, as if he's looking over at the others. Even he, who has never formally met Ian, knows this will cause a stir. "Yes, of course," he finally says.

"Thank you," I say, already nervous. The door to the bathroom opens and Ian steps out. His face is clean-shaven now, and he instantly looks five years younger. He leans against a wall, crossing his arms over his chest. "I've got to go now. Thank you again, Nial, for everything."

"See you soon, Alivia."

I hang up the phone and just take a second to stare at Ian.

In our relationship, it feels as if everything is in chunks of *before* and *after* his death. Everything was easier *before*, complicated, but easier. And then everything was so hard and painful *after*.

Ian stands there, looking just as he did *before*.

I stand and cross the room, placing my hands on his hips before letting my lips find his once more.

I still can't believe we're back here. Allowed to do this without so much pain.

I'll never take advantage of it.

"You ready?" I say as I back away just slightly. Ian nods, and we walk out the door.

A light rain has picked up, and it darkens my shoulders as we cross the parking lot to our rental car. And I revel in the smell of it. The scent of trees that hangs in the air, the mountains that stretch into the valley. It sparks so many memories.

"Head east," I tell Ian as he backs out of the parking stall and pulls onto the road. One step at a time, I guide him across town. Past my old work. Past my old high school. Down the street where my mom taught me to drive.

"Left here," I say. Ian turns and we drive half a block. "This building."

Ian turns into the parking lot and my brows furrow in confusion. The lot is completely empty. Trash is blown up against the building. There's a broken window on one of the upper floors.

Ian parks and I climb out, still observing the obviously vacant building. Finally, my eyes find the foreclosed sign in one of the windows. "What the hell?" I breathe.

"What is this place, Liv?" Ian asks, his hands stuffed into his pockets as he walks forward with me. I walk to the front door of the lobby.

"It's my old apartment building," I say as I try the door. Of course, it's locked. "This is where I lived right before I came to Silent Bend."

I take a few steps back, my eyes going to the window on the middle floor, the second to last on the right. There's a faint, almost undetectable glow in it.

I step forward, cupping my hands around my eyes as I peer into the windows on the bottom floor. Empty rooms filled with only insignificant items left behind. Dirty, stained carpet, slightly damaged walls. But every one of the apartments is abandoned.

"From the smells, I'd guess it's been about five months since anyone lived here," Ian says as he, too, studies the building. His jacket grows darker as the rain continues to fall on us.

I shake my head. "I had no idea the building was in trouble when I moved out. There are sixteen units in this building. It's weird it would just shut down like this."

"Sometimes you just never know," Ian observes. His eyes have fixed on the window with the light on inside.

"It was never a nice place," I say as I walk around the back of the building. "The rent was cheap. The landlord never fixed much of anything. Guess that should have been an indication."

Ian follows me around back. There's a ladder that climbs up the back of the building and connects with the little, wobbly balcony that stretches along the back on the second and third floors. I grab hold of the first, wet, cold, slippery rung and pull myself up.

"What are you doing?" Ian asks. But still, he doesn't hesitate in following me up the ladder.

"That light that was on is in my old apartment." I break through the opening and climb onto the balcony. I walk back two units, to the second to last door. The wood around the lock is slightly splintered. I push gently against it, and it swings open without any fight.

Horror washes through me.

A smear of red brushes across the ceiling in the living area. A splash of it stretches from one wall to the other. The carpet is saturated with blood. Footprints walk through it, going into the bathroom.

"Holy shit," Ian breathes. "Liv, look."

On the old desk that I left in the corner, because I couldn't even give the piece of crap away, stands two pictures. One of my mother, the same one that was displayed at her funeral and in the obituary. And another of me. Taken when I was in high school. I was in a dress, my hair done up in an elegant twist that Mom had done. I'm smiling.

It's a picture I don't recognize, one I know Mom didn't take. It's at an odd angle, as if taken from some distance.

"Who took this?" I breathe as I step forward and pick up the picture. I hover my fingers over the bloody fingerprints on the edge of the picture. I have to take this back to Silent Bend and have Luke run the prints.

"Looks like someone has been watching you far longer than you ever thought," Ian says. He looks over my shoulder, studying the picture of my younger self.

My eyes turn back to the apartment. There are two little LED lights on the desk, set thoughtfully before the pictures, almost as if this is a memorial. There was thought to it, caring.

But there's so much blood here. More than I think one person is capable of holding in their body.

More than one person met their death here.

But *why* were they here?

"You said Jasmine had your mom dug up," Ian says as he walks around the room, smelling for clues. "One of her

Bitten must have come here, looking for who knows what."

"But who did this to them?" I say in horror. I follow the bloody footprints into the bathroom. There's blood smeared over the counter, a handprint on the mirror. I walk back out into the living area. "I mean, the place should have been abandoned by then. Who would use this level of violence to get someone out of a deserted apartment?"

"It certainly isn't a coincidence that it happened in *your* apartment, Liv." Ian shakes his head.

My eyes turn back to the photo in my hand.

I came here as my last stop on the road to closing and reopening the door. I've been searching for my old self, trying to remind myself who I once was, and make a new person. But every stop has been more difficult than I expected.

But this one... I don't know what all of this means.

But there's a cold cube of ice sliding down my spine.

I look back at the small shrine.

"I think we should go," I breathe. I grab the other picture, the one of my mom. "Come on."

"You sure?" Ian asks. "Cause there's something weird going on here, Liv. I don't like the looks of this. This feels...threatening."

I shake my head as I go to the back door and pull it open again. "Doesn't matter. I just need to get home now."

I climb down the ladder again and make a beeline for the car. I wait anxiously in my seat until Ian sits once more, as well. I pull the burner phone from my pocket and dial a phone number.

"We're ready to go," I bark into the phone. "What time will the plane be ready?" I wait patiently for the answer. "Five-thirty. You sure you can't be ready earlier?" I let out a breath of frustration. "Okay, five will do. Thank you."

I hang up and look out the window.

"Liv, you want to tell me what's going on?" Ian asks as he looks from the road to me. "You know something you're not saying?"

"No." I shake my head and watch the dark town I grew up in fall behind as we head back for the hotel. "I'm just finished here. It's time to go home."

Maybe Ian says something in response, maybe he sits there in silence, I don't hear a thing as my mind reels. I don't feel present when we pull into the parking lot once again. My mind is over a thousand miles away. Racing through possibilities.

It's three in the morning. We have two hours to pack and get back to the airport.

All we have to pack our clothes and newly acquired belongings in are plastic shopping bags. But I'm not even aware of what I'm grabbing and stuffing. I'm not even sure I have everything when I find myself staring out the window.

"Liv," Ian says. He walks up from behind and grabs my upper arms. "What's going on?"

I shake my head. "Nothing," I breathe. I blink five times, fast, clearing the fog from my head. "You ready?"

"Yeah," he says, sounding slightly frustrated. He takes a step back and goes to grab the bags.

Together, we walk down to the lobby where I check out and pay the bill. Silently, we climb back into the car and start toward the airport.

Ian keeps looking over at me, concern obvious on his face. I try to offer him a smile, to show him that I am okay. But I'm sure it's not convincing.

We get to the airport early, so when we get the rental car returned, we have forty minutes to sit and wait until the plane is ready for takeoff.

Finally the hatch opens and a worker rolls a set of stairs up to the aircraft.

"Welcome, Miss Ryan, Mr. Ward," a friendly flight attendant greets us. "We'll be ready for takeoff shortly."

I nod my thanks to her. I sink into a comfortable seat and try not to fidget. Ian takes the seat next to me and places a calm hand over my anxious one.

CHAPTER TWENTY-TWO

HUNDREDS OF MILES PASS BENEATH us in a flash. It feels as if I just blinked when we land outside of town, a half hour away from Silent Bend.

It's bright when the wheels touch down. I pull the sun goggles from their box and hand Ian a pair.

"We're so glad you could fly with us this morning," the attendant says with a pleasant smile. She's trying hard to act normal with us wearing sunglasses in the dark airplane, but her smile is just a little too tight.

I offer her a distracted smile and walk down the stairs. Waiting for us just off to the side, in my red Jeep, is Samuel. The second he sees us, he steps forward and takes my plastic bags from me.

"Hey," he says tensely as his eyes flick up to Ian descending the stairs. But he doesn't say anything else. He's at a loss for words at the moment.

"It's good to see you," I say as a hint of a genuine smile comes to my lips. I wrap my arms around him, pulling him into a tight hug.

Samuel remains stiff, and I can just feel his eyes on Ian. But neither of them says anything.

"Thanks for coming to pick us up," I say as I release him and turn back to the car. I pop the back hatch and the bags are piled in. I climb into the driver's seat without asking Samuel for the keys.

Awkwardly, Samuel and Ian do a little dance of figuring out who will take the passenger seat and who has to sit in the cramped back seat. I'm somewhat grateful when Ian just climbs in back without a fight.

"Your face seems to have healed up okay," Samuel says uncomfortably. He rests his elbow in the window, scratching his chin with two fingers. The tension in the air is enough to choke me.

"Yeah," I say distractedly. I'm trying to decide just how fast I can drive without getting pulled over. I couldn't handle any delays. "Did someone call Rath?"

Samuel nods. "He didn't seem particularly willing to come back. But he should get there around the same time we do."

I nod and press just a little harder on the gas.

While our flight flew by, the drive back to Silent Bend seems to take forever. I keep looking at the speedometer, expecting it to be creeping slower and slower. But I'm only gaining speed.

Finally, the familiar little dirt roads crop up. The turn off to Daphne's house. The familiar roads leading to rundown houses and expansive properties. It seems a miracle the snow is all gone. Spring is evident in the blooming trees, in the colorful flowers. It is the end of April.

But as Nial said, there's something in the air. Something with a dark edge. Something tense and terrifying. It crawls along my skin like a thousand tiny spiders, creeping up under my sleeve, hooking on to my chest. Sucking the happiness from my veins.

"You feel that?" I ask as I look back at Ian in the mirror.

"Yeah," he responds simply. "This isn't over."

"Things are pretty well put back together," Samuel says. He watches his town roll by. "But things are tense. Town doesn't know if they trust us, if they're eternally grateful for everything we've been doing to fix their houses, repair the roads, all of it, or if they blame us for how everything feels, just...doom and gloom."

I shake my head. It's all been such an uphill battle. I've been trying so hard for so many months now to win the trust of the citizens of Silent Bend. But this Army just keeps going and screwing everything up.

Finally, we reach the turnoff that leads to the Conrath Estate. My heart races faster and faster as I catch sight of a black SUV just a little ahead of us. It turns at the gates to the property and I'm positive it's Rath.

I'm terrified for what I'm going to find in just a few minutes. But almost as terrifying is facing Rath once more. He left me because I turned my back on everything my father stood for.

And now, I have to beg him to come back. To ask for his forgiveness. To convince him that I am changed.

I pull right up behind Rath and we go through the gates, nose to tail. A breath of relief floods my lungs as the familiar trees that dot the drive surround me. As I observe the expansive grounds that stretch beyond. And finally, when the top of my home comes into view.

The last bay of the garage opens, and Rath pulls straight in. I glide into the space beside him.

Together, the four of us climb out of the two vehicles.

I can hardly look Rath in the eyes. There's too much weight. Too much shame.

"Thank you for coming," I say quietly. But I say no more. Because at this moment, I have something else to attend to. I walk past him and open the door in to the house.

It smells delicious and looks surprisingly clean. When I round the corner to walk past the kitchen, I see Katina working. I catch a glimpse of Beth as she heads toward the rooms on the opposite side of the house.

Since the King has left, the staff has returned.

"Alivia," Nial says in pleasant surprise. "Welcome home."

"Thank you," I say. A crowd stands behind him. My

entire house. But there's a new face. One I've never seen, but one I have no doubt the name of. Obasi. My fellow prisoner at the King's castle.

But I'm distracted. Unable to give a proper greeting to the gathering House members. My eyes are fixed on the doors that let out onto the back veranda as I cross the hall, and enter the ballroom.

My skin instantly warms as I step from the shadows of the veranda and out onto the stone pathway that stretches toward the river. Were I not wearing my sun goggles, I would be blind, in an incredible amount of pain. The sun shines brilliantly, the earth bathed in a white wash of spring warmth.

My heart beats faster and faster as I get closer to my destination.

I can't be right. There's no possible way.

A sweat breaks out onto my palms.

"Liv, what are you doing?" Ian's voice asks behind me.

I glance over my shoulder to see a small crowd has followed me. Ian. Rath. Samuel and Nial. In some ways, I need to face this alone. In other ways, I'm too terrified of what I fear I will find.

I slow as I approach the short fence that surrounds the tiny graveyard. I swing the gate open and take two slow steps forward.

"Alivia?" Rath asks.

But my eyes are focused. Fixed.

Here lies my blood family.

My uncle, murdered by the people of Silent Bend over one hundred and forty years ago.

My mother, taken from this life too soon in such a flawed, human way.

And Henry.

I'm sure my heart is going to leap from my chest, up my throat, and land frantically pounding on the grass at my feet. My palms are slick and my mouth feels dry.

I take the final two steps and lay my hand on the stone engraved with my father's name.

Henry Conrath.

I press my ear to the stone, listening.

Someone takes another step toward me. Rath or Ian, I'm not sure.

But a rock drops into my stomach.

I back away just slightly. My eyes growing slightly wider.

My fingers come to the edge of the opening. I find just barely enough of a ledge to gain purchase with my fingers.

"Alivia, what are you-" Rath asks in horror, but someone cuts him off.

Gathering my recently gained strength, I yank toward me with all my might. A great popping sound echoes as I break the seal. A rush of cold air hits me as I set the stone on the grass.

A few gasps and more than a few curse words slip from every one of my spectators as I stand. And as my eyes come to rest on the inside of my father's tomb, every one of my internal organs disappear.

The inside of the vault is empty. No coffin. No bones or decaying flesh. No traces of Henry Conrath.

But lying flat on the stone is a gold chain, and connected to it rests a pendant. I pick it up, my fingers brushing over the cold metal.

It's my family's crest. The raven at the center. The laurel encircling it, and the crown that sits atop.

But sitting in the center of the raven, is an oddly shaped hole.

My fingers rise to my chest, to grasp the chain that already hangs around my neck.

Panic rises in my blood as I turn. I push my way through the crowd, who are full of questions and shock and disbelief and theories. Rath who is red in the face and tears in his eyes. I run past them all, my body a blur as I race back to the door I just exited.

My footsteps echo as I walk across the marble floor of the ballroom. My eyes fix on the crest inlaid in the floor as I pull the chain from my neck, releasing the key my father left me in a letter when I very first arrived in Silent Bend.

There, where the raven's eye would be, lies a small hole in the marble. I nearly twisted my ankle in it just two months ago at Cyrus' ball. I thought it was damaged, a chip in the otherwise perfect floor.

I sink to my knees as my audience follows me in,

others coming to see what is the cause of all of this commotion.

But I don't see them. I don't hear them.

My hand shakes as I hold up the skeleton key. Quivers all the harder as I lower it.

The tip of the key slips easily into the hole. Sinks in for a moment.

It fits perfectly.

Finally, I look up at those that surround me. Nearly the entire House now surrounds me. Watching me with either curiosity or disbelief. Shocked faces and confusion.

I twist the key, and it gives a heavy click. Something pops, and suddenly there's a grinding sound, coming deep from beneath the floor. *Click. Click. Click.*

Suddenly, the shape of the laurel that surrounds the raven gives a jerk, and I drop five inches.

I'm sinking, lowering. The air suddenly smells sterile. Cold.

Shouts and gasps of surprise sound around me. My eyes rise up to those that watch as I continue to sink.

But finally, they meet Rath's. And the expression on his face tells me everything. He's never seen this before. Had no clue of its existence.

For just a brief moment, I'm back in my old apartment.

The blood.

The violence.

But most importantly, that little shrine to my mother and me.

The reverence it held.

"Rath," I breathe as I continue to slowly sink, "I think Henry is still alive."

THE END OF BOOK FOUR

About the Author

Keary Taylor is the USA TODAY bestselling author of over forty titles, encompassing paranormal, sci-fi, and contemporary romance. She grew up along the foothills of the Rocky Mountains where, from a young age, she started creating imaginary worlds and daring characters who always fell in love. She now lives on a tiny island in the Pacific Northwest with her husband and their children. She continues to have an overactive imagination that frequently keeps her up at night.

To learn more about Keary and her writing process, please visit www.KearyTaylor.com.

facebook.com/kearytaylor

instagram.com/authorkearytaylor

bookbub.com/authors/keary-taylor

tiktok.com/@kearytaylor

Made in the USA
Middletown, DE
16 December 2023